12|21|12

With Special Thanks to Cicely and Dan

Preface

The world ends for someone every day. One day it will end for everyone.

The Smartest Man on the Planet

Dr. Philip Loeb was a theoretical mathematician. He had always said, without pretension of modesty, that he was the smartest man on the planet. At eighteen, he earned his first Ph.D. in mathematics, and three years later, a second in astrophysics. He published his first scholarly work at the age of fifteen and his first best seller, "One Galaxy" at twenty-one. His rise to fame was meteoric, and with it came myriad honors and memberships in every major scientific society in the world. The university where he was employed provided him with a spacious office, a full professorship, a token course load of one honors class a semester, free lodging, and a salary that was a king's ransom.

But for all his intelligence and all his fame, Dr. Philip Loeb could not make the trains run on time. His was late that day and he had missed his connecting flight to Philadelphia for a scientific conference at which he was to lecture. "We Are Not Alone" — that was the title he had given it to attract more interest — but in truth it was a dry dissertation on the technical aspects of faster-than-light space travel. That was his specialty — the mathematics of the folding of space and time.

For many years, Loeb and most of the scientific community believed it more likely than not that life existed on other worlds throughout the universe. The 2011 discovery by NASA of planet Kepler-22b had all but closed that discussion. It was the first known planet in the universe other than Earth where liquid water could exist on its surface and where the temperatures were earthlike, and therefore, where human life could exist. NASA had already cataloged a thousand others like it since the Kepler-22b discovery, but, as exciting as this was, it would neither lead to further government funding nor to manned explorations. The reason was simple — Kepler-22b, the closest of them, was a staggering six hundred light years away.

But Loeb's theories changed all that. Uncovering the secret to folding space and time made the distance between worlds meaningless and time irrelevant. The six hundred light years of space between Earth and Kepler-22b could simply be folded over, and man would be there in an instant. He could even be there yesterday if he so chose, strike a match, return to Earth, and watch it ignite six hundred years from today. That was the paradox of space and time. If he was right, and Loeb always was, faster-than-light travel would recapture the imaginations and purse strings of a public that had lost its taste for riding the carousel of expensive and boring unmanned missions. The brass ring was a virtually limitless universe of raw materials for whoever got to them first, countless worlds for a desperately overpopulated planet to expand into, and who knows how many intelligent civilizations waiting to become the world's next customers.

The possibilities were endless, but the one that fascinated Loeb, and the one for which he was publicly ridiculed, was that some other civilization already knew the secret, and they had found us before we found them. It was only logical. Life-sustaining planets have existed for billions of years, modern day Earth humans for a mere two hundred thousand. If we were on the verge of discovering the secret of faster-than-light travel, would it not follow that a planet with even a one or two hundred-year head start on us would already know it?

That kind of thinking did not sit well with most people. Somewhere in its brief history the human race had acquired a belief that it alone was chosen to rule the world, and once worlds beyond Earth were discovered, to rule them as well. Loeb's intimation that things might be otherwise was heresy and became an embarrassment to the university. That kind of talk put him in the same category as every other crackpot claiming to have seen a UFO or a creature from another planet. He was no better than the nutcase who said he was abducted by aliens and probed and genetically altered before being returned to his family. The university was forced into damage control mode. Loeb was not required to recant outright, but if he wanted to continue in their employ, he needed to equivocate, become more ambiguous on the subject, withdraw from the public eye for a time, and above all stay out of the papers. Loeb did all that, but it did not change his conviction that Earth was being visited on a regular basis by a higher intelligence.

The airline agent was very accommodating. She had read his first book and enjoyed it because it was the first science book she could understand, and she liked the pictures. She got him to autograph his worthless plane ticket for her while she found an alternate flight on a helicopter that would get him to his destination sooner because it would land on the roof of the conference center, not twenty miles away at the airport. Loeb didn't like flying and he particularly didn't like flying in helicopters. They made him sick to his stomach for hours afterwards.

This was what was on his mind that particular afternoon as he neared the conclusion of his lecture.

"Given the data obtained from recent discoveries with respect to creating an infinitesimal black hole under laboratory conditions and given the calculated gravitation pull on the space within the event horizon of the created singularity, and if you properly interpret these equations I have developed from that data, it becomes clear that faster-than-light speeds can be achieved by the folding of space and possibly time as well."

At exactly 12:21:12 p.m. the slide with his equations on it rippled like a pebble in a pond. His hands shook, and he felt sick to his stomach. His heart pounded on his eardrums. Loeb closed his eyes, the moment passed, and he refocused on his notes. When he looked up again to ask if anyone had any questions, he found the auditorium empty. A minute ago, the room's three hundred seats had been filled with coughing, sneezing, throat clearing attendees pretending to understand theoretical mathematics. Now they were all gone, not gotten up and walked out on him gone — he would have heard that.

And not up in a puff of smoke gone — he would have seen that and smelled it. No, they had simply vanished, as had everyone else in the conference center, and everyone else on the street outside, and everyone in every other place he looked. Gone.

He panicked, but panic gave way to questions and hypotheses. For Loeb, the world had always been about solving equations and plugging in numbers. The world's number was not up, one simple fact told him otherwise — not everyone had vanished. He had not. Therefore, it was not the end. Therefore, there had to be others, people with something in common, some factor he had not yet perceived, something that kept them and him from being swept away into the cosmic trash can with the rest of humanity.

He tried to contact his colleagues and friends around the globe. Web servers were up. The Internet was functioning. He had five bars on his phone. Everything was working, but no one was answering. Loeb wandered the city streets. It seemed normal enough: traffic lights told him when to walk and when to wait, tinny holiday music enticed him to come into the department stores for some last-minute shopping, and neon signs seared their impressions into his brain so that he would remember to tell his friends over dinner that night. But a snarl of stalled cars and busses filled every street on every block as if everyone in the city had simply shut off their engines and left.

Near City Hall, Loeb stopped at a newsstand. Under a portable radio spilling static into the frigid afternoon was wedged the last copy of the *Daily News*. Its headline filled the front page: "12|21|12" — the time of the event, the time the human race had vanished, but it was also the date, today's date. Boxed in red off to one side were the top stories: "Doomsday Today — details on page 6, Mayan Calendar Predicts End of the World — exclusive photos on page 4, Mayor to Attend Post-apocalyptic Open House — find this and other fun things to do in the Weekend Section."

He had forgotten. It was the last day on the Mayan calendar, the day the latest gaggle of honking doomsayers and fortune-tellers had proclaimed to be mankind's last on Earth. For weeks, the media had made a circus of it, turning TV into a barrage of inane talk shows and special reports discussing the pseudo-science of Armageddon. Magazines, papers, the Internet, his students — there was no escaping it. Of course, the scientific community and every rational being on the planet dismissed the notion, but they, too, were having fun with it. It was Mardi Gras in December, but he had forgotten because it was ridiculous. There was not a day that went by that was not predicted by somebody to be the end of days. Eventually, one of them would be right. This? This was something else.

Loeb returned to the Freedom Hotel where he had booked a room for the three-day conference. That was where he stayed whenever he traveled to Philadelphia. The lobby was a mausoleum. He took the elevator to his floor and walked down an empty hall past numbered vacant tombs. A room service cart stood abandoned at the door beside his. The eggs were cold but the coffee in the insulated carafe still hot. He took the plate of toast, the coffee, and a half-filled snifter of brandy and locked the door behind him.

The city was beautiful at night. He had always liked the view from the hotel — a ribbon of lights in perpetual motion on the tree-lined Parkway, the illuminated and majestic Art Museum in the distance. The streetlights still converged to a distant vanishing point, but the cars were dark and motionless, and the ribbon gone. He placed the food and drink on top of a magazine on the writing desk by his window. A shot of brandy, then another — the world was falling apart, had fallen apart. He needed to think straight. He needed coffee, coffee and more brandy.

Below his hotel window, the fountain in Logan Circle was dark, its lights and water shut off for the winter. Streetlamps cast the snow-covered park in pale yellow. The traffic circle connecting the

Parkway to all the major avenues in that part of the city had a park where people met and connected — networked, as people liked to say. It was all about making connections. Loeb saw what needed to be done as clearly as he saw the bottom of the brandy snifter.

Priority one was survival. That was a given. Every winter, too many neglected and homeless people froze to death on the streets of Philadelphia. He wasn't going to end up like that. The Freedom Hotel had power and heat, a high-end men's clothing store on the mezzanine, a five-star restaurant, chillers stocked with meat and vegetables, and a passable wine cellar. He would take inventory the next day and get whatever was lacking from the city's finest markets and liquor stores nearby. He would live in luxury to the end.

Finding the other survivors was priority number two. Loeb would not accept that everyone but him had vanished. Millions, perhaps even billions, might have— that he could conceive in a world filled with weapons of mass destruction — but not everyone. Neither species extinction nor the laws of physics worked that way. Physical equations were never solved without some degree of uncertainty. Ask Heisenberg. There are no absolutes in life. And beyond the physical impossibility of such an instantaneous mass extinction, even the smartest man on the planet did not have that high an opinion of himself to believe that, of the 6.8 billion humans, he alone had been selected by nature to survive. There had to be others.

As predicted by the many who feared rather than embraced artificial intelligence, the world's network of computers survived the demise of man. The Internet was the closest thing to a living, thinking being Loeb had found thus far. It chose appropriate ads for him to see as he probed for others online. It knew he was at the Freedom Hotel, suggesting a wine to try with dinner that night. It somehow surmised that he would be interested in a vacation on some remote island near the equator, someplace warm, and it offered to book him an ocean cruise to get there. It even concluded that he needed a date that night.

He posted messages on bulletin boards, giving his email, cell, city, and identity. He posted on hundreds of news sites and purchased ads that automated servers pushed to every major online news outlet on the planet. Everything was connected. TV stations were still broadcasting, most looping endlessly through commercials targeted at a demographic no longer there. Some were transmitting blank screens, which Loeb found more appropriate, but one — Channel Three — was different and so became his inspiration. Its story was an eerie newsroom still life with vacant anchor's chair. This story needed a face, his face.

Days passed before Loeb ventured outside. He chose a cold clear morning to make his way to the studios of Channel Three through desolate streets and around abandoned vehicles. Had humanity at least shown the courtesy of pulling over before the end, he could have driven there, but they must have had more pressing concerns at 12:21:12 p.m. on 12|21|12. He found a bicycle and pedaled the twenty blocks to Channel Three.

No one was there, yet the building seemed alive when Loeb came through its revolving doors. With the station's unmistakable theme music as the backdrop, monitors throughout the lobby ran clips of news broadcasts from history — the first man on the moon, the fateful Dallas motorcade, the boxing match that stunned the world — stories so famous that sound was irrelevant. Motion sensors detected his presence, and an automated greeting welcomed Loeb and asked him to check in with the receptionist. Frozen in time, Friday's closing prices rolled across a stock market ticker above the elevator. The directory beside it told Loeb what he needed to know. He found his way into the electronic heart of the station and set up the recording equipment, sat in the anchor's chair and recorded his message.

"I am Dr. Philip Loeb. If you are seeing this, you are one of the few left. As far as I can tell, everyone else is gone. It's like this all over the city and, in all likelihood, the world. I don't know the cause. I don't know how it happened. It just... did. The systems in place before this event are still functioning: we still have power, heat, and there is enough food to last the winter. The Internet is working, and the satellites are still transmitting. If you are watching this message, know that you are not alone. We must join together. We need to make plans. We need to survive. Contact me. My phone, email, and location are on the screen. Please, contact me. It is our only hope."

He set the station to broadcast at full wattage and tied it into the national network. The tape would loop infinitely. Loeb streamed it over the station's website and linked to it from every video hosting site he could find. He created his own login to the station's billing and tracking software. He couldn't track TV viewers, but if someone watched the video on the Web, he would know. The message was there for everyone to see. Now, all he could do was wait.

Loeb arrived back at the Freedom Hotel when the long afternoon shadows were washing the streets with bitter cold. The world hadn't yet noticed the absence of man. It would be hundreds, maybe thousands of years before the effects of human folly were erased from the planet, but far less before everything shut down and the world came grinding to a halt. Time was "x," the unknown variable in the next equation to be solved.

Fate had not left him a graduate assistant to do his grunt work, so after one stiff drink, and then another to take the chill off, Loeb settled into the chair at his desk by the window and began checking for replies to his posts, comments on his ads, or any sign to indicate someone else was out there.

It came very simply as a soft ping and the appearance of a "1" in the view counter beside his video. Someone else *was* out there. Someone had watched the video. Someone had heard his message. He checked his cell, checked his email — nothing — just that solitary "1" on the computer screen. It stared at him for hours.

Loeb was awakened from a dreamless sleep by music, a song he despised. In the "before" time, he had chosen it as his ringtone for someone not in his cell's phonebook, someone unknown and therefore not worth his time. He cursed the phone, pressing all the wrong buttons before the call went to voicemail.

Night had come to the city. The Parkway was beautiful at night. He had always thought that but had never really taken the time to appreciate it when time was not the issue. Now, with time the *only* issue, he connected to his voicemail. There was one message. He recognized the voice, a woman he had met once, an admirer of sorts, someone infatuated with his mind as well as his body. "Call me, Philip," she said simply. "You know the number." He stared at the phone. The date stamp was two weeks old. He had been in the airport and was tired of waiting in the security line to be screened. He had ignored the call then as he often did. One view, one missed call, no message —the commercials, the test patterns, and his recording played over and over.

The smartest man on the planet realized he was also the hungriest. He showered, dressed, took the elevator down to the restaurant, put on a CD from the collection behind the maître d's station, and listened to classical music while making dinner. What his cooking lacked in culinary skill, he more than made up for with a bottle of wine from the Freedom's cellar. Loeb was drinking the last of it when the out-of-place intruded — the sound of a door opening and a chill gust of air from the lobby.

The Survivalist

Bowen closed his eyes and listened to the helicopter blades chopping the air above. He saw everything: the gleam of the sun on the craft as it dropped below the clouds, its shadow moving across the bright snow-covered hills, the faces of the passengers in the windows looking down at the pristine forest. He saw it all. He had acquired his inner vision from Little Feather, the old Apache tracker. He had lived with him for a year in the wilds. Little Feather taught him about the forest, about people, about life and death.

Bowen opened his eyes when he heard the first crunch. The waiting was over. The buck was eating the apples laid out on a tree stump next to his hide. Thick falling snow was forming a white ridge on the animal's back as it stood motionless and alert. Once the six-point whitetail determined that it was safe, the doe and the young ones hiding in the nearby brush would follow. They were beautiful creatures. Bowen was not hunting them. He had been waiting in his hide in the woods for hours for no other reason than to be close enough to touch one.

Bowen was a survivalist who lived in the mountainous forests of Western Maryland. He offered classes on the subject to anyone willing to shell out $2,000 for a week in the wilds. If they were good enough, students learned how to start fires with a bow drill, how to find their way without a compass, and how to endure their own purification in a sweat lodge. He had written two books on the subject and had become something of a celebrity after tracking down and rescuing a lost child in the mountains, succeeding where the National Guard, a team of trackers with dogs, and an implanted GPS had failed.

Over the years, his business had grown to a staff of five and his lone cabin into a complex protected by ten-foot razor wire and security cameras. There was a mess hall, a dorm with heat and running water (so the paying customers who were learning how to survive off the land could come back at night to a hot shower and a warm critter-free bed), and several hundred acres of real wilderness.

It was four days before Christmas and this was the last class before a two-week break. Bowen was more than looking forward to it. He could smell it as clearly as the musk of the nervous buck beside him. Bowen, the man who made his living teaching others to survive without society, was going to spend his vacation with a woman who never set foot outside the city, the only person in the world he cared about — Carmen. Theirs was an intermittent and unusual relationship, but that was Bowen.

He had taken the group a day's walk from camp and taught them to build shelters to survive the night. Most fared pretty well. The class exercise this last day was to sneak up on a deer and get close enough to touch it. Bowen was waiting there for them. The class was still several hundred yards away, laboring closer behind their camouflage, but making far too much noise. Soon the deer would decide that the danger of the unfamiliar sounds outweighed the temptation of the apples, and class would be dismissed. He closed his eyes and thought of Carmen, of the scent of her perfume and the milky softness of her skin.

The deer bolted, and three crows were flushed from their roost by a loud crack. He heard the student swearing as the deer disappeared over a rise, and he imagined the crows winging off, becoming mere black specks on a vivid winter sky. But the vision was wrong — his class was no longer in it — the crunching twigs, the soft whispers, the rustling leaves were gone, and at 12:21:12 p.m. on 12|21|12 silence spread through the forest like the panic of a student as he was spun around blindfolded and told to find his way back to camp without the use of his eyes.

Bowen searched for his class. He found where they had been. He found signs of all eight of them. He found the last blade of grass one had crushed in an effort to sneak closer to the deer, but he found no tracks leading away, no bodies, no blood. They had simply vanished.

Bowen was not a religious man. His parents had raised him in the church. He couldn't remember which. It didn't matter. They believed in a God who would return to judge the world and he did not. What he believed in were signs, in cause and effect, and for him, life was simply a trail that man followed to its end.

He hiked until dark and built his shelter against an outcropping of rock on a steep hillside with a view of the valley. The forest was home to many animals in winter, yet Bowen hadn't seen a single one since leaving his hide. Whatever happened to his students had scared them all off. There was no sleep for Bowen that night.

He returned to the complex the next morning and found his staff and students gone. They were there one moment and gone the next, just like his class. Outside his office, a boot print and a spidery pattern in the snow told Bowen that someone had been bending over tying his shoelaces when he'd vanished. In the mess hall, he saw where a group sat down at the table, had been enjoying their midday meal, and then were gone. Everywhere he searched, the effect was the same. The cause was unknown and there was no trail.

Bowen picked over some cold food in the mess hall, weighing his options. He called Carmen several times and left messages. There was no answer at either the Ranger Station, the police in the town on the other side of the mountain, or the Maryland Highway Patrol. He spent the rest of the day packing from a mental list of what to bring to the end of the world. That was what his instincts told him he was facing. Whatever had happened in the woods was just the beginning.

Bowen's repeated phone calls to Carmen went unanswered, but he stuck to his plan — pack the Rover, get to the city, pick up Carmen, and drive as far south as his gas would take them. If they could make it as far as the Carolinas... He knew a place on the water down there, a nice place. It would be tough on her, but they would survive, and if they ran into any trouble along the way, he was ready.

He set out the next day, thinking he was prepared for anything. He always had been, but nothing could have prepared him for what he found beyond the camp. Towns, suburbs, cities — everyone was gone without a trace, simply gone. He continued eastward around Baltimore. Stalled vehicles clogged the beltway, turning his trip into a journey of detours and off-road treks. The closer he got to his destination, the worse it became. Bowen finally had to abandon the Rover in a snarl of vehicles just outside Philadelphia. He hoofed it those last few miles through the biting cold. They would survive. It would just be that much harder.

When Bowen pushed open the lobby doors to the Freedom Hotel, he was met by the scent of cooked meat and the faint odor of a man's cologne. He checked his pistol and followed the sound of violins to the restaurant. The curtained glass door opened with a soft rush of air. A man stood up and faced him, his napkin dropping to the floor.

"Who are you?"

"I'm Loeb, Dr. Philip Loeb. Thank God, I knew there had to be others. You saw my message?"

"There aren't any others. Just me."

"How did you find me?"

"I'm not here for you. I came for Carmen."

"There's no one else. I checked every floor." Loeb produced a card key from his wallet. "Here, take it. It's the master key. See for yourself."

Bowen glanced at the key and refocused on Loeb.

"Would you like something to eat perhaps?" Loeb continued. "I can put a plate together and have it ready for you when you return."

Bowen raised his gun. "I don't think so."

"You're going to shoot me? Six billion people vanish from the planet and you're going to shoot me? What kind of imbecile are you? Look around, man. Everyone's gone."

"You're not."

"And you're not either. Don't you see? There must be others. We have to find them. We need a plan."

"I've got my own plan." Bowen waved his gun, directing Loeb to the door. "Let's go."

They got off the elevator on ten, and Loeb opened Carmen's door. The room was empty. A makeup box lay scattered on the sink in the bathroom. Bowen picked up a lipstick. It was hers. Everything in the room still carried her scent.

"This is where she was when it happened." He holstered his gun and sat down. A photo of them together taken last year stared at him from the dresser.

Loeb handed him his cell phone. "Call her. The phones are still working. Perhaps she's just not here."

Bowen looked across the room at a jeweled purse lying on the bed, and punched the numbers into the phone. A sad tune began playing inside it. He tossed the cell back to Loeb. "Have a nice life, what's left of it."

"Wait, you're going to leave? Just like that?"

"Yeah, just like that."

"But our chances of survival are better if we work together."

Loeb followed him to the elevator where Bowen pressed the down button. "You're fat, stupid, and lazy. I'd say your chances of survival are zero."

"But I have shelter with heat, water, power, and food — enough to last the winter at least."

"Really? What kind of heat have you got?"

"Oil. The tank was half full two days ago when I checked."

"So a smart guy like you has already figured out from the manifests how often they used to get deliveries here, right? And a guy with your genius IQ would have already shut off heat to non-essential parts of the building to make what oil he's got last longer, right? Stop me if I'm wrong. And I suppose Dr. Philip Loeb has located a fuel company nearby and knows how to drive their tanker truck here through totally blocked streets when the oil runs out... right?"

"I... I've considered those things."

"I'll bet."

The elevator call button dinged and the doors opened. Bowen got in, and Loeb followed him, staying as far away from his scowl as possible.

"I really think you should reconsider this. Have something to eat. Stay the night. Sleep on it, and let me know what you think in the morning."

"You don't want to know what I think."

"But I do."

"I think if you stay here, you'll be dead in a month."

The doors opened onto the lobby. A man dressed in black was standing in their way. Bowen drew his gun and fired once into the air.

"For God's sake, don't shoot!" the man cried.

The Man in Black

Michael was an ordained minister with no congregation, a failed marriage, and two kids who couldn't stand the sight of him anymore. He lacked conviction in his beliefs and himself, and had lost his sense of purpose. Life hadn't always been that way — in fact, it had been wonderful — but when Michael was diagnosed with lung cancer caused by too many years of too many cigarettes, he lost faith, and with faith went hope, and then love. His had become a miserable existence, and trying to save others was pointless when he couldn't even save himself. Michael, the powerful archangel of God, the leader of the Lord's forces, was nothing like God or his angel, or anything that was holy or good anymore.

He wasn't sure why he continued the treatments. He was dying. The doctors had told him that. Yet every week in the middle of the night he went on an insurance-funded four-hour trip by train to keep a 6:30 a.m. appointment with doctors who did their best to prolong his worthless life. He was sicker than usual after this last one. They offered to keep him overnight, but Michael refused, having long ago resolved that he would not exhale his final breath into an oxygen mask in a hospital, connected to machines by tubes and wires. They found him an ambulance to the airport and a quick flight home.

The irony was that he was praying when the end came, praying that it would all just be over, and that God would show mercy and put him out of his misery. He was in church. He didn't want to be, but he was. He wanted to be in bed, but it was Friday. The church couldn't afford a cleaning service anymore, so every Friday Michael cleaned. It was one of the few things he still did religiously, one of the things the church still let him do. He hated cleaning as much as he hated life.

He had stopped for a minute to let a coughing spasm pass when he saw what he thought was a flash of light outside, and on 12|21|12 at exactly 12:21:12 p.m. the Reverend Michael Costa understood. This was the end. This was God's reckoning, and God had judged the world guilty. He had taken everyone away, everyone but Michael, because Michael was the one person who knew that we didn't go to hell for our sins. Hell came to us.

The world fell out of kilter as Michael struggled the five blocks into the center of town past abandoned cars, the steaming hot dog stand, and the empty bus station. An overwhelming and oppressive quiet had settled over the town. The pizza place, the barbershop, the news agency, everywhere he looked — no one was there. His lungs ached and his coughing brought up blood. Michael gave up the search and limped home.

He turned on the TV and clicked through the stations looking for something, anything.

"I am Dr. Philip Loeb. If you are seeing this, you are one of the few left. As far as I can tell, everyone else is gone. It's like this all over the city…"

When the message repeated, Michael wrote down the phone number and email address of this man who was sharing his hell. He dialed the number.

"Leave your message at the tone if you must."

Michael hung up and then threw up, and then passed out on the floor.

When he awoke, it was getting dark outside. By his watch, days had passed. Michael packed his suitcase, filled his coat pockets with granola bars, the only thing he'd been able to stomach lately, and drove to the train station in the next town. The station was empty as was the train that arrived ten minutes later without a conductor. Its doors opened. He got on board and sat down. The bell rang. The doors closed, and the train accelerated toward the city.

An hour later, Michael got off at the platform below Seventeenth Street, and the train clattered off into the twilit tunnel. On the street, the light changed at the intersection, but the cars did not move. No one sat on his horn. No one ran the red light. There was no yelling, no pushing and shoving, nothing. He tried calling the man in the message again, but the skyscrapers blocked the signal. Logan Circle was the closest open space. He walked the one block there and had begun to dial Loeb's number when he heard music coming from the Freedom Hotel. On any other day he wouldn't have noticed, but on this day he did.

Michael entered the lobby through the glass doors and stopped at the elevators. The floor indicator above the middle elevator was moving from ten, to nine, to eight... It pinged softly when the "L" lit up. The doors opened and a man drew a gun and fired.

"For God's sake, don't shoot!" Michael dropped the suitcase, gripped his chest, and collapsed onto the cold marble floor.

He awoke under a blanket on a bed. The air was warm and heavy with men's aftershave. He heard muffled voices from the next room. It was morning. The cold gray sky was thick with clouds. A man appeared at the door.

"You're Dr. Philip Loeb." Michael sat up. The pain had subsided. "I saw you on TV."

"Loeb will do. And you are?"

"Michael. Michael Costa."

"You're a priest?"

"Minister. There was a man with a gun."

"That's Bowen. He was just leaving when you showed up. Your timing was rather fortuitous as it turns out. He's decided to stay."

"Are there others?"

"Just we three, but I am convinced there are more. How did you get here?"

"I live about an hour west of the city by train. The trains are running themselves."

"Interesting, and possibly useful. How did you find us? I didn't name the hotel in the message."

"I was just trying to get my cell to work. I was going to call you." Michael tested his legs. "I've haven't felt this good in months."

"Don't get your hopes up. Bowen gave you a shot of morphine. There's breakfast in the other room. We'll be waiting."

Michael joined them and ate while they studied a map. "What are you looking for?" he asked.

"There," Bowen pointed. "In those mountains."

Michael looked over his shoulder. "What's there?"

"Camp David," said Loeb. "Mr. Bowen has convinced me that our current situation is untenable. The logical alternative is the presidential retreat at Camp David. It's self-sustaining and designed to be isolated for up to a year in case of extreme emergency. More importantly, there is a top-secret underground train there that can take us to the capital. With the main roads impassable, it may be the only way to get to Washington, and if anyone is still left who knows what happened, that's where they'll be."

"How did you know about the tunnel if it's top secret? Do you work for the government?"

"Hardly. There is very little that can be hidden from public scrutiny anymore if you know what you're looking for. There's a maze of secret tunnels and trains that connects every major installation in the capital. It has been under construction since the Civil War. I've seen old photographs of it. The Pentagon, the FBI, Andrews Air Force Base, Langley, even the presidential retreat here in these mountains are all connected to allow continued operation of the government in a case of extreme emergency."

"It's about 180 miles or so." Bowen stroked his beard. "Holy boy here will never make it back to the Rover on foot. I say we try the same train he took and get west of the gridlock, grab a new set of wheels and as much gas as we can carry, and head west. We can take the turnpike if it's clear. That's the quickest way. We go south here," he pointed. "With any luck, we can be there before dark." He glared at Loeb, "You'd better be right about this."

"Mr. Bowen, if I'm wrong, and I'm not, you may feel free to leave us there and continue on to wherever you wish to go."

While Bowen and Michael packed provisions for the trip, Loeb logged into the Channel Three servers and switched tapes. He had recorded several messages in anticipation of all possibilities, in case he had to move locations. When the indicator showed the new message in place, he switched on the TV.

"...If you are watching this message, know that you are not alone..."

Before turning off the computer, he checked the video's hit counter. It was still a "1," but that "1" blinked hopefully. Now they were three, and there was at least one other human being who had gotten the message. That made four.

The men made their way to Seventeenth and the Boulevard and found the underground platform. The train, as yet oblivious to man's disappearance, arrived right on schedule.

As they pulled into the last stop, Michael looked out on the snow-covered woods. "All my life I'd been taught to think that we were put here to be stewards of this world, but the truth is, the world doesn't need us to take care of it. It was just fine before us and will be again long after we're gone. We're no more than parasites, insects sucking on its lifeblood, killing it a little every day."

Bowen tossed him his bag. "It took the end of the world for you to figure that out? Maybe if we get lucky and survive this, you can preach *that* from your holy pulpit and somebody will listen next time."

Bowen found a vehicle in the parking lot with the key still in the ignition. They filled up at a gas station, packed several more five-gallon gas cans in the back, and headed west. The turnpike turned out to be easy going. Traffic had been light through the sparsely populated mountains west of the city at 12:21:12 p.m. They turned south off the main highway and onto the snow-covered backcountry roads of the Maryland State Forest.

It was while winding around a mountain that they saw the creature — a mass of fur lumbering south. Loeb dismissed it as a bear. Bowen said it was no bear — too upright, too slow. It was something else. He stopped, and it crossed the road into the woods. When he eased forward, the creature spotted them and ran. Bowen stopped the truck and jumped out. "Hey!" he shouted and fired a single shot.

The Creature

He kept to himself and liked it that way. He'd lived alone for as long as he could remember, and with his looks, it wasn't hard to see why — flat nose, scraggily mustache and beard, and a face that could only be described as a ferret's. Until 12:21:12 p.m. on 12|21|12, that's what everyone in town called him — Ferret. He lived in a run-down trail cabin in the mountainous state forest and survived off the town's garbage. In better weather you could find him there every week or so trash picking. He was harmless enough. In the past, he'd had a few run-ins with the law, but he never hurt anyone. He never bothered anyone. He just wanted to get by, just like everyone else. It got so people pretty much ignored him. Some even put food out for him in slings hung in the trees too high to attract curious bears. To many, he was the town mascot, just another oddity that they talked about around the pickle barrel in the general store.

In winter, the mountains were difficult and carried a lot of snow, and Ferret made the trek to town less frequently, sometimes only once a month, sometimes less. He might not have known anything was wrong for months. He might not have realized the end had come until the next time he'd gone to town for supplies. But he didn't have to go anywhere to find out. The end came to him as the sky and forest around him caught fire, and a ball of flame exploded against the side of his cabin. That damn Army must have been testing something in the woods. That had to be it. Who else could it be? Every once in a while they flew recon over his place. They were always up to something, snooping around like that, and now they'd screwed up big time and blew up his damn house.

Ferret remembered little after that. Something in his addled brain told him to run, so he did. He wandered south in a daze, fleeing the inferno with nothing but his coat and hat. The numbing cold drove him to seek shelter in the nearby town. The dumpster behind the lumberyard would be good enough. He could stay in it until he figured out what to do next. And there was always enough scrap wood to make a fire if it got that cold. He would avoid the guard dogs and scrounge for food at night. Ferret was clever that way, but he was confused and lost. He walked for hours, maybe days. He didn't know how many. He was cold, tired, and hungry. He wasn't going to make it to town. He had no idea where town was anymore, and he didn't much care.

A black beast appeared out of the fog on the road behind him and growled. Ferret stopped, hoping it would go away, but it kept coming closer. He crossed the road, and the beast became them, the Army. What had happened was no accident. It was no test. They had blown up his house on purpose. They wanted him dead. They had missed, and now they'd come back to finish the job. Ferret took off for the woods. He heard a shout from behind, then a shot, then nothing.

The Speechwriter

Cameron was twenty-three, and if asked about his graduation from Georgetown less than a year ago, he would say it was due only to the vagaries of rounding. It wasn't that he was stupid or lazy. He was a student of great potential, but he put little or no effort into anything that didn't interest him, and for Cameron, anything was nearly everything, including getting passing grades. The one exception was his writing, and into that he put all his energies.

He had been out celebrating with friends one night after graduation, and on a trip to the restroom he found himself standing in a stall next to none other than the President of the United States. With two Secret Service agents standing guard outside and another watching from over by the sink, Cameron and the president went about their business, staring at the wall, never looking at each other until Cameron finally said, "I thought your speech last night on proliferation was a little heavy-handed, like General Patton had written it. You'll never get anywhere with rhetoric like that, Mr. President."

"And I suppose you could do better?"

"I could do better using words of three syllables or less."

Few can claim that their first successful job interview was held in a men's room stall, fewer still that in less than five minutes they matriculated from unemployed college graduate to the youngest speechwriter for the most powerful leader on Earth, but that's what Cameron did. And now, when the president spoke in the name of freedom and dignity, it was Cameron speaking, maybe not entirely his thoughts, but certainly his words. And whenever the president talked about democracy and the rights of all people to live in peace, that was Cameron, too.

The president was spending Christmas at home that year. That meant the White House staff could observe the holiday with their families or accept his generous offer of a week's stay at the Camp David retreat. The barracks and all facilities would be kept open and available for their use, and they could indulge themselves in amenities normally reserved for guests and foreign dignitaries. Of course, the Marine detachment would remain on duty to make sure it didn't become too merry a Christmas.

Cameron had chosen to spend his holiday at Camp David, but not for the parties. He loved the presidential retreat, loved his walks in the woods, loved the quiet and the atmosphere, but, above all, he loved the time it gave him to write about important things, things he thought the president might want to hear when they took up business again.

On 12|21|12 at 12:21:12 p.m. he was alone with his thoughts as usual and looking out the window. Cameron had always been a loner. Every time he went home his parents asked him if he was seeing anyone, but he never was. Whenever his friends asked him to go out, he almost never did. It wasn't that he didn't have the opportunity for a relationship. He'd had plenty of opportunities, just never the inclination.

A blinding flash filled the sky, and the room jolted as if tossed into the air, throwing Cameron against the wall. Lights flickered, then came back on. The backup generators kicked in. It could be but one thing — a nuclear attack — and that was the initial shock wave emanating from Washington. Only one country had the capability of delivering such a strike on the capital, but why now after such successful disarmament talks? And why no warning? Was it a dirty bomb —a nuclear weapon brought into the country in pieces and assembled by terrorists at ground zero? They had been briefed on that. The yield would have to be enormous to reach into the mountains seventy miles away. Could a terrorist build such a large bomb? The shelter was on the other side of the Camp David compound under the barracks. Cameron stopped thinking and ran.

Into the cold afternoon and through the compound, past quiet buildings and across the main road where a black SUV sat with its door open, he ran. Panic urged him on faster. Everyone else was already in the shelter. If they followed procedures, and they always did, they would close and lock the blast doors. They wouldn't wait for stragglers. They wouldn't wait for him. Camp David was a beautiful rustic retreat nestled in the pristine forests of Maryland, the perfect place to think and write, but in minutes it would all be gone in a nuclear firestorm and him with it if he didn't get inside.

Into the barracks, down the stairs, into the red dusk of the steel and concrete shelter — Cameron closed and locked the doors behind him. He was inside. He was safe. He was alone. There were no orders being issued by cooler heads, no panicked cries, no despair, no footsteps running on the metal walkway to the elevator, and no one pounding frantically on the doors to get in. He switched on the outside monitor. The barracks were empty.

The thought of going back for the others who hadn't the sense to run for cover crossed Cameron's mind, as did the futility of adding another glowing dead body to the radioactive pile. Instead, he broke the rules. He unlocked the steel-reinforced doors before descending into the safety of the solid rock of the Appalachian Mountains.

Cameron hated elevators. He hated confined spaces, but he hated the alternative more. The elevator let him off at its only stop — the nuclear strike-hardened shelter three hundred feet below the surface. Built to be self-sustaining for up to a year, it had its own power and underground water source, and there was enough food for a hundred people for a year or, in his case, one person for a hundred years. No one else had made it. No one.

The command center was a square concrete room where dozens of computers registered information about the compound and all in-house systems. He waited there for that inevitable moment when the screens would flash with a light so bright it would blind him, but that moment never came.

Hours passed. The external monitors showed no radiation, no anomalies, nothing. All security systems and cameras throughout the compound and on the perimeter seemed to be working. The only odd thing was the one thing they weren't registering — everyone else.

He tried to contact the Marine captain of the guard, the Secret Service, the FBI, the Pentagon, the CIA, the president. He tried his parents and even his old college roommate. Camp David was connected to every major capital in the world. The lines were open, but no one was answering. This was no surprise nuclear attack. Cameron's life was his words, but he had no words for this.

Days passed before Cameron ventured above ground. It was Christmas. He walked to the edge of the compound. Snow was falling on the quiet woods. He held a short note he had written while underground:

Dear Mom and Dad,

I'm so sorry I didn't come home this Christmas. I wish now I had. I tried to call, but there was no answer. I miss you all very much. Merry Christmas.

Love,

Don

Cameron read the note one last time and dropped it into the snow.

He was near the gatehouse on his way to the lodge when he heard a car. A black vehicle crested the hill and crashed through the gate, turning right at the crossroad. It passed the camp commander's quarters and pulled up at the dispensary. The driver and a passenger got out of the front and pulled someone from the backseat, helping him up the steps and into the building. When Cameron got to the car, he found a man in the back unconscious, a minister. He had started for the dispensary door when the man on the seat awoke.

"Don't," Michael said. "Bowen will shoot you. Hit the horn, then put your hands over your head and wait with me."

Cameron turned to run. The shelter wasn't that far. He would escape these backwoods lunatics and lock himself in. They would go away.

"For God's sake don't, please. He'll kill you." Michael leaned forward and fell on the horn.

Bowen heard the sound and left Loeb with the man named Ferret. He drew his gun and went outside. When Cameron saw him, he put his hands over his head.

Bowen aimed his weapon. "Stop right there. Who are you?"

"Don't shoot. My name is Cameron. I'm not armed."

"What the hell are you doing here?"

"I work for the president."

"Is there anybody else?"

Cameron shook his head. "Just me."

Camp David

The four men sat on easy chairs in front of the gas fireplace in the lodge's great room. Ferret, his head wrapped in a bandage, was asleep on a sofa.

"And that's how we three met." The wineglass hummed as Loeb ran his finger around its rim. "We encountered Ferret quite by accident on the way here. Apparently, he's a vagrant who lives off the trash from a town in the vicinity. I'm not a medical doctor, but I believe he'll be fine. Fortunately for Mr. Ferret, Bowen is not a very good shot."

"If I was trying to hit him, he'd be dead."

"So," Loeb set his glass on the table. "Now we know each other's stories."

"Where is everyone, Dr. Loeb?" Cameron asked. "What happened?"

"Uncertain, but it's like this everywhere."

"You tell us. You're the president's boy." Bowen downed his scotch and crushed the ice cube between his teeth.

"Do you mind?" Loeb said.

"Mind what?"

"Chewing your ice. It's very annoying, like scraping your fingernails on a chalkboard."

"Just my luck: the end of the world, and I get stuck with my mother." Bowen got up and poured himself another drink.

"I don't know anything, Mr. Bowen. I just write speeches. It doesn't make any sense. They're gone... just gone. I've tried everyone: the White House, D.C. police, CIA, other countries, even the president's private number. There's no one there."

Bowen adjusted his holster and sat down again. "We're here. You're here. Explain that."

"Do I even remotely look like I have a clue? I'm not a scientist. I'm a speechwriter. Dr. Loeb, what happened?"

Loeb's gaze wandered out the window. "Camp David is quite beautiful in a rustic way. It has a wonderful history dating back to the late 1930s. Did you know that President Eisenhower renamed it 'Camp David' in honor of both his father and grandson?"

"Dr. Loeb?"

"Yes, of course. You would like to know what happened, wouldn't you? At precisely 12:21:12 p.m. on 12|21|12, the world as we know it ceased to exist. The exact day the Mayan calendar ended — incredible coincidence, don't you think?"

"You don't really believe that, do you? That's the same as people in 1999 saying 2000 was going to be the end of the world because PCs stored the year as a two-digit number. Don't you think it's more likely the Mayan carver just ran out of space on his calendar wheel?"

"What do you mean?" Michael asked.

"I mean, maybe the Mayans should have had Macs. They're good till the year 3000, right? I don't know. I'm just saying that nobody predicts the end of the world with a calendar. It's like saying Hallmark controls our destiny."

"How *does* someone predict the end of days, then?"

"With fire and brimstone like they do in the Bible, or maybe they tweet it, or put it on their Facebook page. I have no idea. Come on, Dr. Loeb. Tell us. You were the *Enquirer*'s poster boy. That *was* you on the cover a few months back with your arm around that three-headed alien, wasn't it? What's going on?"

Loeb winced. "It's amazing how little it takes to turn scientific inquiry into a three-ring circus."

"So was it Mayans, or aliens, or what? Because I, for one, would really like to know."

Michael put his hand on Cameron's shoulder: "Take it easy, son. We're all doing the best we can under the circumstances."

"Circumstances? What circumstances? Didn't you say just a little while ago in our meet-and-greet that hell has come to us? That's what you said, right? What's there to understand about that? They burn you on one side and flip you over to do the other."

"Cameron," Loeb said. "Get a hold of yourself. I've never believed in doomsayers, Mayan or otherwise, and I refuse to believe that we have been visited by a supreme entity holding the Bible in one hand and eternal damnation in the other. There has to be some logical explanation for this."

"But you said yourself it was an incredible coincidence. So what is it, really?"

"Face it, kid," Bowen said. "Loeb is just as clueless as the rest of us. It's the end of the world. Just deal with it." He emptied his glass. "Damn, that's fine scotch."

"If you can explain to me how we are discussing the end of the world *after* it has ended, I will certainly entertain the notion," Loeb said. "But Bowen is right about one thing — the president does know how to stock a bar."

The Christmas tree twinkled in red, yellow, and green. A pile of brown dried-up spruce needles covered the carpet underneath. Cameron unplugged the lights. "Do you think there are any others like us out there?"

"I've thought so from the beginning, and we are the living proof of that. There must be other pockets of civilization gathering just as we have. We need to find them. We have to join forces if mankind is to survive. It's our only hope."

Bowen crunched another ice cube between his teeth. "What for? They could all turn out to be like whack-job over there. Why bother with the rest when we can live here like kings for a hundred years?"

Ferret stirred, mumbled something incoherent, and went back to his fitful snoring sleep.

"God is punishing us," Michael whispered.

Loeb poured himself another glass of champagne. "Don't be ridiculous. God does not punish people with fifty-year old single malt scotch and Dom Perignon. Cameron, is there caviar by any chance? I read somewhere that the president fancied it."

Michael drew on his bottle of water, suppressing a cough. "Wine is a mocker, strong drink a brawler, and whoever is led astray by it is not wise. Proverbs 20:1."

This trip, Bowen brought the bottle back with him. "Yeah? Well get this — shut the hell up. No wants to hear your crap anymore, you religious prick. Bowen, chapter one, verse one."

"We are being punished for our sins, Mr. Bowen."

"I've got no sins, padre. My soul's as lily white as a bedsheet." Bowen lit up a cigar. "Besides, I could get used to this kind of hell."

Cameron had taken a glass ornament from the Christmas tree. He threw it against the wall. "This is crazy. This is like Nero fiddling while he watched Rome burn. Shouldn't we be doing something instead of just sitting here on our thumbs?"

Bowen blew a cloud of cigar smoke in his direction. "Like what?"

"Oh, right. I forgot. This is productive, isn't it — getting drunk and smoking the president's cigars?"

"I don't think he'll mind, boy, do you?"

"Cameron's right." Loeb put his glass down. "We can waste time later. Right now we should focus on finding the others. I need access to your computer center, your phones, the Internet, camp schematics, everything."

"Sure, but I'm telling you there's no one out there. I already tried."

"There's at least one other person out there. We'll start with him."

Cameron and Loeb left the others and went to the command center where Loeb again checked for messages, comments, posts, anything to indicate someone else was out there. The video counter was still a "1." He tapped the keyboard: "Someone viewed the video, but they either can't or won't contact us. What do you make of that, Cameron?"

"How do you know the "1" isn't you? Or maybe it's a computer troll, or something like that."

"Valid question. The software is supposed to filter me out by login, but I hadn't considered the possibility of it being an automated program. Do we have access to the CIA from here, not the one the hackers play with on the Internet, I mean the secure connection?"

Cameron handed him a red folder marked "Top Secret." "I found this in the camp commander's office. It has the daily password from the twenty-first. Last I checked they hadn't changed it. You'll have to use the gray dinosaur over there. It's the only one on the private network."

Loeb clicked through a maze of screens on the isolated computer until he arrived at the CIA secure site.

"What are you doing?" Cameron asked.

"The CIA has access to every phone record, every Web transaction, every click, every view, everything we see or do electronically. And they store it all right here."

"I'm sorry. I guess I missed that on CNN. They track everything we do? Without a warrant? Isn't that somewhat illegal?"

"Don't be naïve. Of course they do. I realized it about three years ago when the technology for ultra-massive storage became affordable even to people like you and I. It was only logical that the CIA had been using it when price was not an issue. Of course, I never went public with my beliefs. I have enough trouble with the media as it is and no desire to end up in a ditch in Rock Creek Park."

"Yeah, that would suck."

The page split into a double screen of Loeb's video on the left and computer gibberish on the right. He ran his finger down the symbols and statements line by line. "There it is. The video was accessed from the backbone of the capital hub on this main trunk. And there is the IP address."

"And that is helpful how?"

Loeb made a face.

"I'm not a geek," Cameron said. "I'm a writer."

"Every computer on the Web has an IP address. That's what makes it possible to send and receive information between distinct individuals over the Internet. Think of it as a phone number. If you know someone's phone number, you can call him. If you don't, you can't."

"So call him."

"He's apparently not online now."

"Who does the number belong to?"

"Therein lies the problem. What do you do when you know a phone number and need to know who it belongs to?"

"Is this a test? I hate tests."

"Do you even own a cell phone, Cameron? You do a reverse lookup, obviously."

"Silly me. Of course you do. Everyone knows that. It's so obvious."

Loeb entered several commands into the computer and waited. "The problem is that not everyone has a static IP address like they do a phone number. When they log into a service provider, that provider assigns them the first available address from the bank of numbers they've purchased. It can be different every time they log in, within the limits of their range of numbers, naturally. That makes it nearly impossible to trace someone who uses a large service provider, unless you also have access to that provider's login records to connect the dots, and thanks to the CIA, we just happen to have that."

"I'm going to nod and pretend I understand every word of what you just said, okay?"

Loeb swiveled the screen so Cameron could see it more clearly. "Whoever watched the video did so from inside the White House."

The Watcher

Loeb raised his glass to the others around the table: "Here's to the holidays: peace and good will to men, at least to what's left of us. If only we had da Vinci to paint this last supper."

He and Cameron had prepared Christmas dinner from the turkey and fixings set aside for the president, had the president chosen to celebrate the holiday there, and, more importantly, had he survived 12|21|12. Michael, bolstered by stronger meds from the dispensary, had been talking nonstop about heaven, hell, and redemption. The more he talked, the more Bowen drank. That was his idea of an anesthetic. Ferret ignored them all.

"What's the matter, Ferret, we're not good enough for you?" Bowen asked.

"You shot me, remember? And you don't smell right."

"I don't smell right? You've had two showers, and you still stink like a skunk, you waste of a bullet."

"I wish I had gone home for Christmas," Cameron said, more to his cloth napkin than anyone in particular. "I miss my parents. I'll never see them again, will I?"

"It wouldn't have mattered, Cameron," Loeb said. "They would still be gone."

"I suppose they would, but then maybe I would, too."

"So we're not good enough for you either?" Bowen's elbow slid off the table, knocking his water glass onto the floor.

"You drink too much, Bowen," Loeb said.

"Yeah, and you talk too much."

"What's going to happen to us?" asked Cameron.

Bowen grunted and waved a thick finger, stirring the fog that had settled around his brain. "We'll grow old and die. Or I'll shoot you. One of the two. You pick."

"No, I mean the human race. Is this it? Are we finished?"

"God has judged us, and found us guilty," Michael coughed. "Repent while there's still time."

"Fine words for a man who's told us he's lost his faith, cheated on his wife, and robbed his church."

"At least I had faith once, Mr. Bowen. What have you got? To you, life is nothing more than survival. The one who deserves to live is the one who's better at taking what he wants from others."

"Damn straight, padre. You see, that's the difference between you and me. I know there's nothing more than this crap, so I can deal with it. You think there's got to be something else, something you're going to miss out on because you screwed up, and you can't handle it. Just remember, everyone goes the same way when they die and that's six feet under. The sooner you realize it, the better off you'll be."

"God left the five of us here for a reason, Mr. Bowen. I believe that now. Everyone is here on Earth for a reason. I'd just lost sight of mine and, God forgive me, I'm sorry for that, but now it's clear to me that the Almighty has left me here to tell you that it's not too late to come to Him and confess your sins."

"If that's your reason for living, padre, you're wasting your time. I've got nothing to confess." Bowen looked into his empty glass. "I've got no reason to be here."

"I know why I'm here. It's because them dumb bastards missed," Ferret laughed. "They blew the crap out of my place, but they didn't get me. No sir. Must not a-been using them expensive smart bombs. Guess they could only afford the dumb ones for the likes of me."

Cameron exhaled. "I write speeches. It's what I do. And they're good speeches. The president thought so... I thought so... Maybe God did pick us for a reason, but why choose me? I don't have the brains of Loeb or the skills of Bowen, or your religion, Michael, or even Ferret's dumb luck. I just write."

"Grace is a gift that no one deserves," whispered Michael.

The oak paneled dining room had seen many a joyous holiday over the years, but it was neither merry nor bright that Christmas. There were no presents under the dead tree and no stockings hung by the chimney. Over the fireplace, an old mantle clock ticked softly. After dinner, Cameron made coffee.

"And that is why God let you live, Cameron," said Loeb. "That's the best cup of coffee I've had in a long time."

"Amen to that," smiled Michael.

"I was a barista at Capital Coffee my junior year. Can you believe it? The pay was lousy, but I got a free coffee IV out of it. It kept me going. I've been thinking, Dr. Loeb..."

"Here we go again," Bowen pushed his chair back. "I'm going to need more scotch and another cigar for this."

"No, seriously, I've been thinking about this. If we do survive, maybe there is a place for a writer like me. Maybe I should chronicle this for future generations."

Ferret slurped the coffee that had spilled into his saucer and wiped his mouth on the linen tablecloth: "Waste not, want not — that's what I always say."

Loeb shuddered. "That's assuming, Cameron, that the human race survives at a level somewhere above Cro-Magnon, I presume?"

"You don't think we're going to make it, do you?" said Cameron.

"Oh, individually we will survive to the end of our days, assuming Bowen doesn't shoot us first, but one thing is crystal clear. We are not, last I checked, an asexual species. If we don't find others, specifically if we don't find any women, our lives and the life of our race will wind down pointlessly, and there will be no future generations to read your chronicles."

Ferret smacked the table. "Now you're talking. I say we each round up as many chippies as we can, screw all day and party all night. Now that's my kind of salvation."

"Ferret?" Loeb said.

"Yeah what, Doc?"

"If it comes to that, I'll shoot you myself."

"Don't you worry Doc, they'll be plenty for everyone."

Outside the window, the night sky was filled with stars, and the moon reflected in pale blue off a fresh covering of snow.

"For the human race to survive, we *must* find the others."

"We've been over this, Doc. The human race is finished."

"I refuse to believe that, Bowen."

"Believe what you want, it's over for us."

"Can we be a little more positive, people? Maybe we should focus on finding the one who viewed your video, Dr. Loeb?"

"Look kid," Bowen scowled. "Don't you think they would have contacted us by now if they could? Face it. They're dead."

"We should at least try."

"Why? What difference does it make? When I die, that's it; the world ends for me. Whatever happens to you losers after that happens. It's no concern of mine. I'll be a dead, rotting corpse."

"That's just cold, Mr. Bowen. We're people just like you. We're your own kind. We should stick together."

"You're nothing like me, boy."

"You'd feel differently if Carmen were here," Loeb said.

"You leave her out of this."

"Who's Carmen?" asked Cameron.

"Mr. Bowen's one and only soft spot, apparently."

"You shut up before I shut you up, you intellectual nobody." Bowen grabbed his bottle and stumbled out of the room.

Loeb raised his glass in a toast and emptied it: "And to all a good night." He dabbed his lips with his napkin and plopped it on the plate. "Well. There you have it. I can solve the most complex equations in the universe and come up with theories to explain anything, but I'll never figure out people, even when there are only four of them left."

"So wait, you *do* have an idea what happened, don't you?" Cameron said. "You're just not saying."

"I am working on a hypothesis, yes, but I don't have enough evidence yet."

"Can't you at least share? It's not like we'd be calling the tabloids with photoshopped high school reunion pictures of you on a pyramid surrounded by aliens or anything."

"It's pure conjecture. I need more data."

"Dr. Loeb, I know I'm only speaking for myself, but I'll take anything at this point."

"Suit yourself. The question is simple: Where are the 6.8 billion people? Answer that and the rest becomes obvious."

Cameron turned to Michael. "Of course! Why didn't *we* think of that?"

"Cameron," Michael said, putting down his teacup. "I know you're just trying to cope with this. We all are, but I'm not sure your sarcasm is helping."

"I'm sorry, I'm just not ready for this... this Armageddon. Maybe if I had more time to prepare, take some notes, brainstorm ideas..."

"Not everything in life is a speech, son. At some point, you just have to accept things and act."

The fireplace was warm and relaxing. Loeb stared into its yellow and orange flames: "You do know that these gas flames are highly inefficient," he said. "But they are designed that way because that's what people expect to see when they looked at a fireplace. It looks more 'real.' We have the technology to make a more efficient gas flame, one with combustion so complete that it would give off little or no emissions, but then the flame would be cold and blue and uninviting. We can't have that, can we?"

Cameron buried his face in his hands. "This is insane. I must be dreaming."

"I've considered that possibility as well," said Loeb. "But ask yourself this: if this is a dream, why can't you wake up? Furthermore, dreams are vague and indistinct constructs of our own experience. They may have the appearance of detail, but they are never this elaborate or this real. And even in my wildest dreams, I would never have included anyone remotely like you, Bowen, or Michael, and certainly not the likes of Ferret. No offense intended, of course."

"None taken. Where is Ferret anyway?"

"He likely went outside to prowl. I saw him at the window a few minutes ago."

Cameron picked out a few songs on the electronic jukebox that was next to the bar.

"You're a little young to be a Beatles fan, aren't you?" Loeb asked.

Cameron listened to the song and stared at Loeb. "What if we're all in the *same* dream?"

"And we're the ones who aren't real? Preposterous."

"But I don't like the Beatles. I have no idea why I picked that song."

"Then who is dreaming?"

"Maybe the one we think watched the video is actually the one who is dreaming, and we're all just ideas rolling around in his head. Maybe that's why we have no control over this, and that's why I picked the Beatles — because he likes the Beatles. That's why we can't wake up. We're not real."

"Cameron, if you truly believe we are no more than a dream in some Beatle lovers head, I don't think there is anything I can say to convince you otherwise, but I choose to go by the facts. And the fact is that billions of human beings were here at one point in time and simply not here the next. I have no proof, but I think the explanation is clear enough."

"It is?"

"Of course. Isn't it obvious? The people are not here because someone took them away."

"What? No way."

"Then tell me, what happened? There are no bodies, no destruction, nothing."

"I don't know, maybe it was one of your alien visitors with a ray gun that just zapped them all into nothingness."

"If one person a minute were removed from this planet, it would take thirteen thousand years. Even at a hundred a minute, it would still take 130 years. I think we would have noticed your alien with a ray gun," Loeb said.

"Maybe it was a really big ray gun and he got them all in one shot, you know, like the Death Star?"

"As I recall that destroyed the planet as well, didn't it?"

"So they've done some upgrading. I don't know. What difference does it make? Everyone's gone, and we're still here."

"It makes all the difference in the world to me. If we assume that whoever is behind this is benevolent and that we were simply left behind, it behooves us to find out if there is still a chance we can rejoin the rest of our race. If, rather, we assume that this was an attack of sorts, we should stop looking now and start hiding."

"Which do you think it is?"

"I would think if another race had eradicated our species in a prelude to colonization that they would already be here, and we would have seen them. On the other hand, if they came for raw materials, they are in for an unpleasant surprise. In either case, we would know they were here. But in my mind, there seems little point to attacking a planet as insignificant as Earth."

"Maybe they came and took everyone to be slaves on their home world."

"Six billion slaves? That's a lot of mouths to feed, and I don't think we're talking about Pharaohs in space ships."

"Maybe they're using us for food."

"If so, wouldn't it make more sense to grow us in our native environment and harvest us here as needed? Cameron, I would be more than happy to discuss any other imaginative speculations you might make, but to answer your question directly, I believe that those who are responsible for this did so with good intentions."

"You mean like to save us? But you said yourself that it would take hundreds or thousands of years. There would have been announcements, meetings, plans... We would have known about it."

"We didn't know about it because it all happened in an instant of our time."

"Okay, that's impossible unless you're now saying you do believe in giant ray guns."

"Actually no, it's not. Space and time are relative, and the only logical explanation for such an event is that whoever did this was able to fold space and time to accomplish a centuries-long task in an instant."

"You mean time travel?"

"That's precisely what I mean."

"So they traveled back to some point in time..."

"12:21:12 p.m. on 12|21|12 to be precise."

"And they gathered up as many people as they could and took them away in their space ships or whatever, and when they came back again..."

"They returned at exactly the same instant of our time and moved another group off the planet."

"So for us, it all seems to happen in that same moment even though it takes them hundreds of their years. That's pretty deep, Dr. Loeb. Is that even possible?"

"Indeed it is — if one were actually able to fold space and time. Then he could be anywhere he chose at any time he chose without having to travel there using more conventional methods."

"So they could have transporters, or a star gate, or something like that?"

"I would assume so."

"Where is it?"

"I don't know."

"So why didn't they take us, Dr. Loeb?"

"If this were an exam and you got five wrong out of 6.8 billion, it would still be an "A." No one is perfect, Cameron."

"So we're a mistake? That's comforting."

"Or perhaps, as the good reverend said, we were left behind for a reason. Perhaps they left us here to gather up the other stragglers."

"So when they came back again they would take us all in one shot on the last bus out of town. That makes sense. We need to find that bus station, Dr. Loeb."

Cameron cleaned up. Loeb went to the computer in the study to continue his search, and Michael retired for the evening. Later, Cameron brought Loeb another pot of coffee.

"Any luck, Dr. Loeb?"

"Not really. The only activity on the Internet is automated. There have been no more views of the video. Nothing."

"I just have one more question. If they were saving us, what do you think they were they saving us from?"

Loeb gave up searching sometime in the middle of the night. He couldn't sleep, and instead wandered the hallways nursing a headache and fighting back the nausea that had been bothering him on and off since that day in the city. He thought about it, and it made no sense: the world spins on its axis at over one thousand miles per hour, orbits the sun at over sixty-seven thousand miles per hour, rotates with the rest of the galaxy around its center at 490,000 miles per hour, and it all travels through infinite space at a staggering two million miles per hour. How was it he felt motion sickness from the simple act of walking?

He stopped to rest in a chair near an archway leading to the other wing of the lodge. A security camera's red light blinked on. It had been dark when he'd first entered. He was sure of it. The camera rotated toward him, and the lens spun to focus. Loeb stood up and waved: "Is anyone there? Hello?"

The light blinked out.

Cameron, Michael, and especially Bowen were less than enthusiastic about being dragged to the north wing second floor hallway by Loeb, but his urgency prevailed. They watched the security camera for several minutes before the light came on again.

"There!" Loeb pointed.

"It must have a motion sensor," Cameron said. "They all do, don't they?"

"Not that I saw, and if it did, why the delay? Where are these monitored?"

"The cameras for the entire compound are monitored continuously from a secure room off the barracks, or at least they were. I can't believe there's anyone still in there. It's been days. There's also a feed into the shelter command center, but no one's there either, Dr. Loeb. No one's anywhere."

"Take us to the monitoring room, Cameron."

"So much for the element of surprise," Bowen waved at the camera. "And you bastards can probably hear every word this dipstick is saying, can't you?"

"There's no microphone, Bowen. I checked."

"This is bullshit, Loeb. It's hooked to a dumb computer just like everything else around here. It has to be. We searched the place. There's nobody here."

"For once, I'm inclined to agree with Mr. Bowen," Michael said. "And, if you'll excuse me, I'm going back to bed. I don't feel well."

"Maybe there are motion sensors around here somewhere, and you just can't find them, Dr. Loeb." Cameron shrugged: "And it is kind of late."

"Perhaps you're right," Loeb agreed.

When they were out of the hall, Loeb motioned them into an alcove. "I'm going to the barracks. The possibility that someone is watching us, but has chosen not to communicate, troubles me. I could use your help for this or your pistol, Mr. Bowen."

Bowen stared at Loeb's outstretched hand. "Yeah, all right, I'll go. Can't sleep anyway."

The four men slipped out of the house through the kitchen and found Ferret there relieving himself in the bushes.

Michael stopped to look at the sky. "Dr. Loeb, I've always thought we were God's chosen people, but when I look up at the stars and realize how small we are, I feel so alone and insignificant."

"There are billions of worlds in the universe, Michael. We're not alone, just very far apart."

A dark stream of clouds trailed across the moon. Cameron framed the sky in his hands: "That's Orion, isn't it? The Hunter?"

Loeb looked up and realized that more was wrong than just 6.8 billion people missing from the planet.

The living room sofa was warm and comfortable. Someone had relit the fire. Electric Christmas candles twinkled in each window of the room. The smell of cinnamon, oranges, and cloves from a potpourri on an end table made Loeb want to vomit. He sat up slowly and focused on Michael, who was sitting opposite him in a chair.

"Feeling better?"

"Yes, thanks. I guess I fainted?"

Michael nodded. "We found the room with all the cameras, but no one was there. Cameron thinks it's being monitored remotely from the White House."

"How long have I been out?"

"Not too long. Would you like some water or something to eat?"

"No. Get the others. Now."

When everyone was there, Loeb began, "We have to get to Washington."

Bowen opened another bottle of scotch. "We've been down that dead end too many times, Doc. What's the point?"

"You're a survivalist, Bowen. The point is survival."

"Finding one more peeping Tom isn't going to change a damn thing. I'm staying here till spring, then I'm heading south."

"It won't do you any good."

"What are you talking about?"

"Cameron asked me earlier what they were saving us from. What indeed? Why spend hundreds, even thousands of years and countless resources transporting every living being off this god-forsaken planet? Why?"

"Who gives a crap? Even if there is a 'they' like you say, 'they' didn't take us. We're stuck here. We're on our own now."

"You'd better hope we're not."

"Look, I don't care if someone is watching us from D.C. It's not going to change a damn thing. You can take your crackpot theories and stick 'em where the sun don't shine. Once the weather breaks I'm out of here."

"Bowen, listen to me. What if I told you that everyone's disappearance was just the beginning, that something terrible is happening right now, something that will make your little jaunt south as meaningless as putting on Coppertone before you're thrown into a blast furnace?"

The ice in Bowen's drink clinked against the side of his glass like a lonely chime on a breezy day.

Loeb looked out the window at the star-filled sky. "Billions of stars and planets, more galaxies than can be counted. Creation really *is* a beautiful thing if you stop to think about it..."

"So what?"

"So, I want to see it one last time through the telescope at the Naval Observatory in Washington."

"Loeb, you've totally lost it. We have to go to D.C. because you want to look at the pretty lights?"

"You're right, Bowen. I have lost it, and if I'm wrong, you can shoot me."

The Tunnel

They found the tunnel in a remote wing of the shelter. A single twelve-passenger electric car sat at the platform facing a concrete tube lit at regular intervals by triangles of dim yellow light.

"According to this map, there's a stop under the National Cathedral. That's where we'll get off. It's only a few blocks from there to the Observatory," Loeb told them. "The long delays, the cost overruns, the eighty-some years of construction — it all makes perfect sense now. They weren't having trouble with the cathedral. They were building this."

The smooth reinforced concrete walls were icy to the touch. Cameron blew into his fist. "This is amazing, Dr. Loeb, and no one has any idea it's here."

"So much for hundred dollar hammers and thousand dollar toilet seats," Ferret said. "I've been saying it for years. All this top secret crap — that's where you're hard-earned tax dollars are going."

The train ran itself after Loeb punched in the instructions to its computer. It was seventy miles to the White House, somewhat less to the Observatory.

"I'm glad you decided to come, Bowen."

"Well, Loeb, it's like this. I've lived in the woods all my life. I've slept in the rain, and I've laid in the mud. And for what?"

Michael patted him on the shoulder: "It's never too late to repent. God understands."

"Who's talking about God? I'm just saying I'm a lousy cook, and I could get used to the whiskey and cigars."

The tunnel angled downward as they left the mountains. It was getting colder, and the heater in the car switched itself on.

"When I was growing up I always wanted to be an astronaut, not a policeman, not a fireman; it was always astronaut," Loeb said. "To fly into outer space and see the stars up close... That was what I always wanted. Then I found out I hated flying. I get airsick. Ironic, isn't it?"

"From astronaut to astrophysicist," Cameron laughed. "I always wanted to be a fireman until I burned my hand on the stove. Then I found out I could write and not get burned so badly or so often. What about you, Ferret? An interesting guy like you, what did you want to be when you were growing up?"

"I wanted to ride the rodeo, be a real cowboy like Roy Rogers."

"Roy Rogers... He was a person? I thought it was just a fast food chain."

"You do realize he was born in Cincinnati?" Loeb pointed out. "And that 'Roy Rogers' wasn't his real name."

"Don't care. Roy was one of the good guys. Always will be."

"Since we're all telling our life stories, what about you, Bowen?" asked Loeb.

"Does it matter now?"

"Don't tell me you grew up with no aspirations other than to stalk the wild asparagus?"

"Loeb, I'll bet that mouth of yours gets you in a lot of trouble."

"No so much any more, actually." Loeb went back to staring out the window at the lights flying by in the tunnel.

"I was in a band in high school. We wanted to be rock stars."

"What made you change your mind, Mr. Bowen?" asked Cameron.

"We sucked, just like every other punk kid band. That's what."

Cameron turned to Michael: "That leaves you. What did you want to be when you were growing up?"

Michael shifted in his seat. "My aunt and uncle were missionaries. I always wanted to be one, too, ever since I was a boy. It was my calling, God's calling. It just didn't work out that way."

"Funny, isn't it, how none of us ended up what we wanted to be?"

"I visited them one summer," Michael went on. "But a rival tribe attacked the village. They didn't like the idea of us converting their neighbors, so they beheaded my uncle and tortured my aunt."

The train bumped over a connection and followed the green signal at the intersection into a wider tunnel on the left.

"They let me live. They sent me home to tell all the others that they would get the same treatment if we ever came back. I never did. I was too afraid. I was just a boy."

"Okay, that's pretty awful. I'm sorry, Michael, I was just making conversation."

"I should have gone, Cameron. It was my calling, and God has been punishing me ever since."

Loeb got up and checked their progress. They were nearly to the Cathedral. "Michael, trust me, God doesn't have to punish us. We do that quite well on our own."

The train pulled into the station under the National Cathedral. The five men got off and made their way up a metal staircase to a locked door that Loeb opened with an access card he had made at Camp David. From there, it led into a vaulted stone hallway and then to a side chapel off the nave.

Michael knelt in front of the altar and began to pray.

Bowen dragged him to his feet. "Save it, padre, I don't think anyone's listening."

They left the church and walked south past darkened buildings to the observatory. Loeb and Bowen located the observatory's backup generator while the others waited. The lights came on, and when the two returned, Loeb was carrying an armful of computer printouts.

"What's that?" Michael asked.

"This forty-foot telescope has a twenty-six inch lens and was once the largest refracting telescope in the world. It's not anymore, of course. Now, the Navy uses it primarily to measure the parameters of double stars — position, angle, separation, and so forth. Every clear night, they take photos of as many of them as they can. There are several they are actively tracking, so those they photograph every night. The photos go directly into the main computer to be analyzed. These are the printouts from the evening of the twentieth. By comparing this data with the photos we'll take in a few moments, I hope to be able to tell you all what exactly is happening."

"I hate to break it do you, Doc," Ferret said, looking up at the telescope eyepiece. It was ten feet off the floor. "But we didn't bring no ladder."

Loeb flipped a switch on the base of the telescope and the entire floor rose up toward the eyepiece. "Gentlemen, I give you the largest elevator in the city of Washington, D.C."

Loeb set the telescope to view the first double star, took the high-speed photos, and left them to get the printouts from the computer room. When he returned with the new data, he was preoccupied and refused to speak with anyone. He checked and rechecked the settings and took another set of photos. He even moved on to the next double star on the list and took several sets of that. When he returned from the computer room the second time, he slumped in a chair with the papers in his lap.

"Well?" Bowen asked.

"I was wrong."

Bowen drew his gun and ran his finger down the barrel. "So I can shoot you now?"

"You may as well. It doesn't make any difference."

"Dr. Loeb, what did you see through the telescope?"

"The end of mankind, Cameron. A gloriously ignominious sight to behold."

Bowen holstered his weapon. "What the hell are you talking about?"

"Back at Camp David, I knew something was wrong. The stars weren't right; more specifically, Mars wasn't right. In the night sky, it should be visible in Aquarius until February at least, but it wasn't in Aquarius."

"Where was it? In Uranus?" Ferret laughed. "Get it? Uranus."

"Somehow, that seems a fitting last joke for the human race."

"Mars has moved?" Cameron asked.

"It appeared so, but it was impossible to tell without this data. I thought it more likely a distortion of the reflected light striking the Earth."

"A distortion? Caused by what?"

"By the one thing possessing a strong enough gravitational field to bend light — a black hole — and this data proves that out. At exactly 12:21:12 p.m. on 12|21|12 our futures were forever altered by a black hole."

"Wouldn't we see something that big coming?

"Not necessarily. All black holes resolve to a point without dimensions, the singularity, and the event horizon, the area of space within its gravitational pull, could be millions of miles across or as small as our planet or much, much smaller. And if it were traveling through the galaxy at a sufficient rate of speed, we might never see it, even when it was upon us."

"But we would have had some warning. The government would know, right?"

"This isn't the movies, Cameron. We aren't constantly watching the skies for objects on a collision course with Earth."

"So where is it?" Bowen asked.

"It's gone."

"Gone? What do you mean gone?"

"The Milky Way is traveling through space at about two million miles per hour, Bowen. Light, about three hundred times that fast. Even assuming the black hole was only going the same speed as our galaxy but in the opposite direction, it would be beyond the sun in a single day. This data indicates it was traveling much, much faster than that, but it came so close that we were within its event horizon for a brief time. Fortunately or unfortunately as the case may be, it could not entirely overcome Earth's inertia before leaving the solar system. Otherwise we would have been sucked in immediately and obliterated, and we wouldn't be having this discussion."

"So you're saying this black hole sucked six billion people off the planet?" Bowen laughed.

Ferret whistled. "That's a powerful lot of sucking, Doc."

"Idiots. Obviously I'm not saying that."

Bowen took a flask from his jacket and took a long pull. "So what *are* you saying?"

"I said that Mars looked like it was in the wrong place in the sky. That was incorrect. Mars is where it should be. It's Earth that is a million miles out of position. Apparently, while we were within the black hole's event horizon, the tremendous pull of its gravity altered our orbit. We're now moving away from the sun at approximately sixty-seven thousand miles per hour and accelerating. Unless our orbit stabilizes soon, at the rate we're accelerating, we have less than a month before the planet's surface becomes uninhabitable. The average surface temperature will drop to minus one hundred degrees Fahrenheit and continue to decline until every living thing left on the planet freezes to death. That is assuming, of course, that we don't run into something like an asteroid or another planet on our way out of the solar system."

The heaters in the observation room couldn't keep up with the falling temperatures outside. Beyond the opening in the roof, dawn was breaking on a world that should have been waking up for the start of another day.

"That's why they took everyone," Cameron whispered. "They knew this was coming."

"See, Doc, I told ya it was them Mayans all along," Ferret said.

"You never said anything of the sort."

"Well, I was thinking it. Don't you see? They figured it out. They saw it coming and got out of Dodge when the getting was good. Then they sent in the cavalry for the rest of us. That's what them UFOs sightings was all about. They weren't Martians. They was Mayans. That's their ship the government's holding at Area 51, the one with all that funny writing on it. It's Mayan, I tell ya."

"Is it possible there was a civilization on this planet that lived so primitively by our standards yet was so advanced that it could predict an extinction-level event two thousand years into the future? And if we allow for that, must we not also allow for the possibility that they were capable of leaving Earth, finding a new home, and coming back to relocate us?"

"That'd make a great bedtime story, Loeb, but what good does it do us? We're dead in a month."

"Oh, we can survive for years underground once we get to shelter, Bowen. Even with the extreme surface temperatures, Earth's core is still molten metal and will continue to generate sufficient heat for our lifetime and beyond if we are far enough underground. We'll be the last of our species, living in a hole in the ground like our ancestors of thousands of years ago. We will end as we began. Fitting."

"Then let's get going. We can be back to Camp David in an hour."

"Bowen, wait. We're forgetting one thing — our friend at the White House."

"He's on his own."

"We're just going to let him die?" asked Cameron.

"We're all going to die, kid. It's just a matter of when."

"No, this is wrong," Michael said. "We need to try and save him."

"I suppose you're going to tell me that it's God's will or something?"

"I don't pretend to know God's will anymore, Mr. Bowen. This is just wrong."

"He's right," Cameron said. "What's the point if we can't live like humans anymore?"

"The point is survival, boy."

"What if he's one of them?" Loeb asked. "He could be the key to this whole thing."

"One of them? If he's one of them, why the hell didn't he say so and point us to the spaceship? This is bullshit, Loeb. There's no aliens, and there's no Mayans, and there's nobody coming to rescue us. I don't know what happened to everybody, and I don't care. But I'm damn sure I'm not going to die a Popsicle out here with you."

"What if he's been telling us to come to the White House all along?"

"Maybe that's where the transporter is," Cameron whispered.

Bowen pushed Cameron aside. "Loeb, have you gotten any messages, any at all, from anyone?"

"Think, man. Whoever took everyone else away must have a mental capacity that is light years ahead of us. What if he's been communicating with us and we just don't understand?"

"I don't hear anybody talking but you, and I'm getting pretty sick of it."

"Would you just listen to me for a minute? Why did you come with us, Bowen? You've wanted to dump me from the first day we met, yet you came with two total strangers to Camp David even though you didn't want to, and you came here with the four of us even though you said it was a bad idea. Why did you do it? Why? Think, man. Something or someone brought the five of us together. You said it yourself — we have nothing in common. You didn't see my messages. You didn't check the Internet. Yet somehow you found me."

"We should at least check it out," Cameron said.

Bowen moved nose to nose with Loeb. "I was looking for Carmen, not you."

"Don't be stupid. You knew she was gone. Everyone else was. And despite what Michael said about God leading him to us, he found us by what seemed to be pure luck."

Bowen glanced over at Michael who just shrugged: "He's right, I was just trying to get a signal for my cell."

"And we just happened to see Ferret crossing the road in the woods? Six billion people vanish from the planet and we just happened to come across one of the five survivors in the middle of nowhere? What are the odds of that?"

Ferret spit on the metal floor through his crooked yellow teeth. "I was freezing my ass off."

"How could all of that have been luck? And what made me choose Camp David in the first place? A hunch, an educated guess that there was a top-secret tunnel with a train connecting it to the White House?"

"So?"

"So, Cameron was there. Think, Bowen. He was sending us to get Cameron before we came to Washington."

"What you're saying is that we're the aliens' escort service, and they send us telepathic waves or something to go pick people up. Right? Loeb, I've heard just about enough of your intellectual crap. You want to go weirdo hunting? Fine. Go ahead. And anyone else who's crazy enough to go with Dr. Nutjob here, be my guest. I'm heading back to Camp David and once I lock that door, I damn sure won't be taking any callers."

They followed Bowen back to the Cathedral and down into the tunnel. The train was gone.

"I think your little space buddy is trying to tell us something, Doc," Ferret said.

"It's seventy miles to Camp David," Loeb said. "It's less than three to the White House. That's where I'm going, if anyone wants to join me."

The White House

The five kept to the walkway running alongside the tracks. Yellow numbers painted on the walls every tenth of a mile were counting down to zero. The world was traveling in the wrong direction and had been since 12:21:12 p.m. on 12|21|12. For Loeb, it was spinning out of control.

"Only a mile to go, Dr. Loeb," Cameron said. "You can make it."

"I don't feel well."

"There's an infirmary there. They'll have something to settle your stomach."

"I hope so. I feel terrible."

"You don't think it's because of the planet shifting, do you?"

"I don't see how. We're already traveling through space at millions of miles an hour. A few thousand more in different direction shouldn't make any difference."

Michael leaned against the wall, soaked in sweat. "I'm not doing so well either. I think the meds are wearing off."

Bowen peered down the tunnel: "Let's go. We ain't got all day."

Loeb took Cameron's offer of a shoulder. "Yes, it wouldn't do to be fashionably late for the end of the world, would it?"

For Loeb, the last mile passed like the final march of a prisoner to the firing squad: inevitability carried him forward, and fear held him back. When the yellow numbers reached zero, they were underneath the White House, where their train was parked at the platform. They entered the maze of whitewashed hallways, passing directories listing briefing rooms, situation rooms, and numbered conference rooms, finally seeing "Monitoring Center" listed among them. They found the infirmary on their way there. They were outside the monitoring center's locked steel doors when a deep-throated rumble passed through the complex like a distant thunderstorm.

"The access card isn't working," said Loeb. "I don't understand. I rekeyed it for full clearance back at Camp David."

"Try it again," Cameron suggested. "Maybe it's a glitch."

"Lick the little brown strip, Doc," Ferret said. "That's what they do in the FoodMart when the cards don't swipe."

"I didn't realize they had card readers on dumpsters, Ferret."

A vibration like the bass turned up too loud rattled the corridor.

Bowen drew his gun. "What the hell was that?"

Something stirred inside the room, and time stopped for the five men. The doors slid apart, releasing the scent of cinnamon, oranges, and cloves into the hall. Into the doorway stepped a woman. She had long black hair and dark olive skin, unnaturally elongated features, and six fingers on one hand. In the other she was holding a device no larger than a cell phone pointed directly at them.

A single shot rang out. The smell of gunpowder filled the corridor, and a dark red stain spread across the woman's chest. The device clattered to the floor, and she collapsed.

Loeb knelt down beside her. "Bowen, what have you done?"

"She was going to shoot. You saw it. It was self-defense."

The woman opened her dark eyes and grasped at Loeb's arm.

"Don't," he said. "Try to stay still."

Ferret picked up what the woman had dropped. "This ain't no ray gun, but it's got a big hole in it where dumb ass here shot it."

"It looked like a gun. I swear." Bowen grabbed the device. The symbols on its keypad meant nothing to him. "It looks like some kind of TV remote."

Cameron knelt down beside them. "We're the ones from Camp David."

She smiled at him and whispered two words.

"What did she say?" asked Bowen.

"It sounded like 'Camp David,'" Cameron said.

"Camp David," she repeated and nodded.

"I'm Cameron. Who are you?"

She smiled and whispered, "Maya..." Pain spread across her face, and she closed her eyes.

"Did she say 'Mayan?'" Michael looked upward. "Thank God. We're saved."

The rumbling began again, and the corridor seemed to roll sideways. Hairline cracks snaked across the walls, and chunks of plaster came crashing to the floor.

"We've got to get out of here," Loeb said.

"What about her?" asked Cameron.

"Leave her," Bowen said. "We'll never make it if we have to carry her."

"We can't just leave her here. She'll die. I'll be right back." Cameron ran off down the hall.

"Who gives a damn about her?" Bowen said. "I say we leave her, get on the train, and get back to Camp David. That was the plan, right?"

A ruptured steam pipe hissed somewhere above a hole in the ceiling.

"It was never the plan to kill innocent people, Bowen."

"Where I come from, she ain't people, Loeb. Just look at her."

"I don't care. I am not a murderer."

Cameron came back with a stretcher, and they lifted her onto it. The complex was coming apart, the corridors collapsing behind them in clouds of broken concrete and drywall as they retraced their steps back to the train. The tunnel there had caved in, and the train was crushed beneath tons of rock and cement.

Bowen found no way around it. "What the hell do we do now?'

"Looks like it's time to bend over and kiss your ass goodbye," Ferret laughed.

"We passed some fire stairs in that last hallway," said Cameron.

The door to the fire stairs gave way with some coaxing from Bowen's foot. The metal steps inside the fire tower were intact, but the block walls were covered with a spider web of stress fractures. Another tremor shook the facility, and the door behind them buckled and crumpled beneath the weight of the concrete. They climbed hundreds of feet to a door at the top and ran into the open from the small block enclosure hidden in some tall bushes on the South Lawn of the White House. A fiery yellow sun glowed high in the sky behind thick rolling clouds, and wind whipped across the open space, lashing at them mercilessly. Devastation was everywhere: massive old trees lay toppled and thrown about like twigs, the east wing of the White House had caved in and smoke was rising from a crater next to it, fires were burning throughout the city. The earth shook again, and the White House groaned as it shifted on its foundation.

Cameron steadied the stretcher. "What's happening, Dr. Loeb?"

"I don't know. This whole area is unstable. We can't stay here."

The woman on the stretcher grabbed his arm. "Camp David," she said.

Loeb showed her the device that had fallen from her hand. "What is this?"

She took it and pressed a few buttons. Nothing happened. She held it out to him and nodded: "Camp David."

A helicopter sat on a pad across the lawn.

"That's our ticket out of here," Bowen said. "Let's go."

"Can you fly that thing?" asked Michael.

"You bet your ass I can."

They made their way through the debris to the helicopter. The sky darkened in disapproval, and the air temperature turned subarctic. The earth rolled in waves underneath their feet, and Loeb's world spun wildly.

"We've got one problem," Bowen said. "That helicopter won't carry all of us. It's a four-seater. We've got too much weight. Unless one of you can fly this thing, you four have to pick which one stays behind. I vote her. She's not going to make it anyway."

"Maya..." she whispered. "Camp David."

"We can't leave her," Loeb said. "It's our fault she's like this, and she's the only one who can save us. Don't you see? She's trying to tell us something about Camp David."

"Like what?"

"Maybe her ship is there, or maybe she has another one of those handhelds. It could be the transporter device. Maybe there are others like her there."

"And maybe you're full of crap. What about the rest of you? What do you say?"

"What good is saving ourselves if we lose our souls?" Michael said. "I'll stay."

Cameron shook his head. "No. I'm not going unless we all go. There has to be a way. Isn't there anything else we can get rid of, like the seats or something like that?"

A fierce wind rocked the helicopter as Bowen cast off the last of the lines. "There's no excess cargo, and we don't have time to unbolt the seats. If we're going to make a run for it, we've got to go now."

"You can't run from this, Mr. Bowen," Cameron said. "We need to do the right thing here."

The woman squeezed Cameron's hand and closed her eyes.

His voice cracked: "As humans, that's all we've got."

They lifted the stretcher onto the helicopter.

Michael shook his head: "I'm dying. Don't you see? It makes perfect sense for me to stay. At least the rest of you have hope."

"This is absurd," Loeb said. "Only one of us has to stay behind, and it should be me."

"The captain going down with his ship? No, I can't let you do that," said Cameron. "It's all or none."

"If you three want to die here, suit yourselves." Bowen started up the helicopter and shouted: "Ferret, you coming?"

A light came on in the Oval Office, and a window over the South Lawn opened. It was Ferret. He waved to them.

"Ferret!" Loeb shouted.

"Look at me, I'm the president of the world!"

"Get down here!"

"No sir, I ain't going in no helicopter and I ain't going in no spaceship. I'll die right here on good old Mother Earth, thank you very much, and there's nothing you can do about it."

"Looks like you've got yourselves a hero," Bowen said. "You others coming or not?"

The temperature was dropping fast and the city crumbling around them as they took off for Camp David, flying low over the trees in Rock Creek Park.

12|21|12

December 21, 2012. 12:15 p.m. Loeb watched an angry storm building to the north as the helicopter flew low over the trees in Rock Creek Park. He didn't like flying and he particularly didn't like flying in helicopters. They made him sick to his stomach for hours afterwards, but he had missed his flight, and it was the only way to get to the conference in time. The world below was a dreary lifeless gray, and the imprint of man had receded behind a thickening drape of snow. The craft thumped over a ridge of high pressure.

"Looks like we're in for some weather," the pilot said over his shoulder.

"Mr. Bowen, how soon will we be in Philadelphia?"

"We have to make a stop near Hagerstown, Doc. A couple hours, I'd say."

The scent of cinnamon, oranges, and cloves filled the cabin. It made Loeb sick to his stomach.

"Can't you do anything about that smell?"

"Ask them. I'm just the pilot, Doc."

Seated next to Loeb was a young clean-cut man in his early twenties. Loeb figured him for a college student or a recent grad. "I'll be getting off there," the man said. "I'm spending Christmas at Camp David. Cameron's the name." He extended his hand. "I'm one of the president's speechwriters. You're Dr. Philip Loeb, aren't you?"

Loeb accepted the handshake. "Yes, is it that obvious?"

"I recognized you from that photo of you with your arm around that three-headed alien."

"Presidential speechwriter — you seem a bit young for that kind of work."

"And that coming from a man who got his first Ph.D. at eighteen?"

"Touché."

"Are you speaking at the conference in Philadelphia, Dr. Loeb?"

"Yes, and if you'll excuse me, I really do need to prepare." Loeb reopened the folder in his lap containing his notes and slides, and went back to reading through his lecture.

Another passenger, bundled up in a black overcoat, adjusted himself in his seat. Cameron turned his attention that way: "Are you all right?"

The man opened his eyes. "I'll be fine, just a little queasy. It's the chemo. I just got out of a treatment."

"Are you going all the way to Philadelphia, too?"

"Yes." He shifted again, and the flap of his coat fell back, exposing his collar.

"Priest?"

"Minister... in my better days. I'm Michael. I'd shake your hand, but I was told I should avoid close personal contact until the effects of the drugs wear off, susceptibility to germs and all that."

There was one other passenger in the four-seater, a black-haired woman with dark olive complexion and thin angular features. She was curled up in her seat watching the others with curiosity. Cameron waved to her and she smiled.

"How about you?" he asked. "What's your story?"

She nodded.

"You're wasting your time. She doesn't speak a word of English," Bowen shouted over the engines. "She's getting off with you, Mr. Cameron. They told me she's one of the new cooks at Camp David."

"Oh, okay. That's cool," Cameron smiled at her again: "I'm Cameron," he gestured. "And you're?"

"Maya," she grinned, pointing to herself. "Camp David," she nodded.

"You have six fingers on one hand. That's different," Cameron said.

Loeb looked up: "The condition is called polydactyly. It's not all that uncommon."

"So, where are you from, Maya?"

She nodded again, "Maya... Camp David..."

The news came on the nine inch TV mounted on the bulkhead above them. "Did any of you happen to catch the president's speech last night?" Cameron asked.

The sky lost definition as the clouds wrapped tighter around them and up and down became the same. The wind stalked them on all sides as the helicopter bucked against a wall of snow.

Loeb grabbed his stomach. "Jesus, Bowen, can't you keep this thing steady?" At exactly 12:21:12 p.m. the slide with his equations on it rippled like a pebble in a pond.

Something exploded against the helicopter. Sparks showered the window, and the craft shook and slammed Cameron against the wall. The lights flickered, then came back on.

Michael sat up straight. "Did you see that?"

Bowen called over his shoulder. "Is everyone okay back there?"

The helicopter lurched and bucked again, tossing into the air anything not tied down. A single shot rang out. The smell of gunpowder filled the cabin.

Loeb picked up a smoking pistol lying on the floor among his notes and papers. "You carry a loaded weapon on a helicopter?"

"Oh, my God!" Michael pointed to Maya. She was holding what looked like a TV remote in her hand pointed directly at them. A dark red stain spread across her coat.

The craft shuddered and spun, and losing forward momentum, it plunged out of the clouds.

Bowen closed his eyes and listened to the helicopter blades chopping the air above. He saw everything: the gleam of the sun on the craft as it dropped below the clouds, its shadow moving across the bright snow-covered hills, the faces of the passengers in the windows looking down at the pristine forest. He saw it all.

Epilogue

On December 21, 2012, a special evening edition of the *Daily News* hit the streets with the simple headline "12|21|12." It was devoted to a series of odd stories and events from a day that some believed would be the end of the world. The top stories were: "Doomsday Today — details on page 6, Mayan Calendar Predicts End of the World — exclusive photos on page 4, Mayor to Attend Post-apocalyptic Open House — find this and other fun things to do in the Weekend Section."

Tucked away between a full-page department store ad and the sports section was this story:

Helicopter Crash in State Forest

December 21, 2012

By Adrienne John-Samuel and Jeni Beske Roberts/Associated Press

Hagerstown, Maryland. A commercial helicopter crashed in a remote section of the Maryland State Forest earlier today. Residents of a nearby town told police they heard a loud noise shortly after noon and reported seeing a plume of black smoke rising from the forest in the area of a nearby abandoned cabin. When the fire department and local police responded, they found the helicopter engulfed in flames and the cabin fully involved. High winds and freezing temperatures hampered efforts to extinguish the blaze, but the fire was declared under control at 1:30 p.m. One firefighter was taken to Hagerstown Hospital for treatment for smoke inhalation and is in satisfactory condition.

The National Transportation Safety Board is investigating the cause of the accident. Their official spokesperson stated, "According to the pilot's flight plan, the helicopter took off from Washington, D.C., at approximately 11:50 a.m. Its destination was the Philadelphia Market Street Heliport with one scheduled stop in Hagerstown, Maryland. Preliminary information obtained from the craft's black box indicates that the helicopter's external sensors registered a sudden drop in temperature around 12:19 p.m. EST. It is not known at this point if the extreme temperatures contributed to the crash, but it should be noted that the helicopter was equipped with an autopilot system. Data shows that it was engaged at the time of the incident. Based on the wreckage pattern and the fact that the bodies of the pilot and the four passengers were not recovered at the scene, state police and federal marshals, in conjunction with the Maryland National Guard, have instituted a rescue and recovery search in a 5-mile radius around the crash site. Identities of the passengers are being withheld pending the results. There have been reports from local authorities of a squatter or squatters living in the cabin, but these reports are unconfirmed. The cabin was directly impacted by the craft's fuselage and burned to the ground. Investigators are on the scene sifting through the rubble and a full report will follow. The NTSB has no comment on reports that no one was aboard the craft at the time of the crash. Further information will be disclosed as this investigation proceeds. Data from the helicopter's black box fixed the time of the crash at 12:21:12 p.m. on 12|21|12."

Works by Larry Enright

If you enjoyed this story, please take a look at my complete works on the following pages. All are available online.

FOUR YEARS
FROM HOME
LARRY ENRIGHT

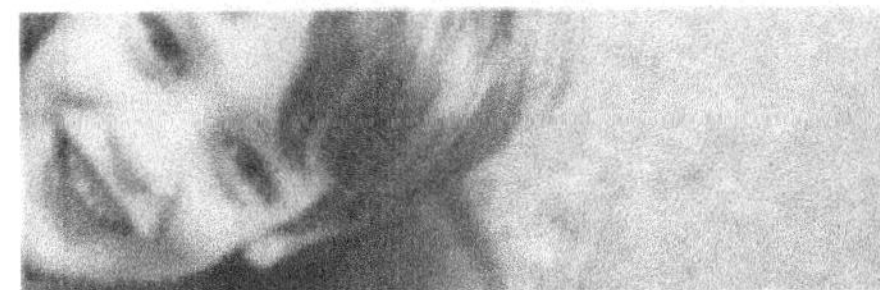

Genre: Psychological Mystery
Published: October, 2010

Four Years from Home is the story of Tom Ryan, the firstborn of five in an Irish Catholic family. Smart and acerbic, he called himself the future king of the Ryans. Harry, the youngest, was the family's shining star. Sensitive, and caring, he was destined for the priesthood until something changed, and he abandoned his vocation. When he left for college, he left for good. He never called. He rarely wrote. It was as if he had ceased to exist and the shining star had been but a passing comet in the night sky.

The story begins on Christmas during Harry's senior year at college. The Ryans have gathered for another bittersweet holiday without Harry. When an unexpected gift arrives, Tom must make a reluctant journey of discovery and self-discovery into a mystery that can only end in tragedy. Four Years from Home defines brotherly love in a darkly humorous and poignant tale told by an unlikable skeptic.

Genre: Literary Fiction/Mystery
Published September,2012

A Cape May Diamond was the recipient of a 2013 Independent Publishers Book Award in eBook fiction. Sequel to the best seller, *Four Years from Home*, it picks up the Tom Ryan story two years after its tragic ending in the discovery of the fate of Tom's youngest brother, Harry. It is not required that you first read Four Years from Home before A Cape May Diamond, since it is recapped in brief in the first chapter of the sequel.

The result of a chance encounter, A Cape May Diamond can best be described as a story of life, love, and a journey of a thousand years.

This is a story of how things never quite work out the way you think. You might find a love story in here somewhere. You might not.

You might find a message hidden in one of the nickel pop bottles collected by the beachcombers from some of the most beautiful white sand beaches in the world. You might even find a little mystery, but life is a mystery, isn't it?

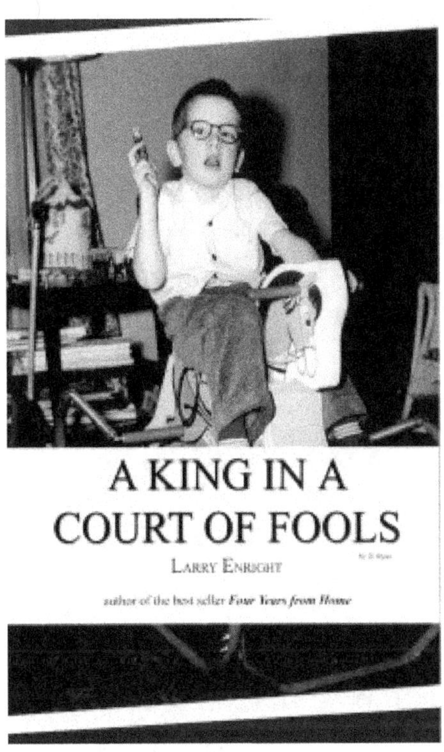

Genre: Nostalgia Fiction, Kid's Mystery (age 6-up)
Published September, 2011

A King in a Court of Fools begins with a book — The Book of Tom — a journal writing assignment from Tom Ryan's sixth-grade teacher, Sister Jeanne Lorette. That's what she called it. Tom called it punishment. In it, he chronicles the adventures of the Caswell Gang, a group of siblings and friends with two things in common — their love of adventure and their allegiance to Tom, their king.

The 1950s book was misplaced a long time ago, and all the children have since grown up, but Harry, Tom's youngest brother, still remembers it and retells for us one of its stories in a nostalgic, heartwarming, and humorous way that will have you wishing for adventure, too.

Genre: Christmas story for kids of all ages
Published November, 2011

Buffalo Nickel Christmas is the story of a special day. It begins with an ordinary boy in an ordinary world, but as a monster storm approaches, and Christmas Eve finally arrives, the boy discovers that he is anything but ordinary, and that the world is a very magical place indeed.

You will meet some unusual people and hear unbelievable things. You might even see a wizard and a king or two. Sixteen forevers will pass in this book. That's a very long time, and many magical things can happen when it's sixteen forevers and still no Christmas. Whatever you do, don't listen to that little voice inside your head that tells you it's illogical, that it doesn't make sense. Listen for the whistling teakettle and be ready with your wish.

Genre: Science Fiction/Literary Fiction
Published March, 2012

12|21|12 - The world ends for someone every day. One day it will end for everyone.

Genre: Science Fiction
Published: October, 2013

Walter Stickle is a creature of consistency: from the time he gets up, to the clothes he wears, the food he eats, the way he works, how he spends his free time . . . He does everything the same way. Every day. Boring? Maybe, but he likes his routine. It's normal. But Walter also likes the Galactic Rangers. He reads the comic strip. He collects the action figures. He goes to the ComicCons. He is obsessed with them. Why? Because despite the sense of security he finds in being normal, Walter has always dreamed of going to the stars. Just once, he would like an adventure. Just once, he would like to be the hero. If only hc had the chance.

Our story begins with an ordinary man, an anomalous pair of mismatched socks, and a comic strip. It ends with the adventure of a lifetime.

Genre: Science Fiction
Published: July, 2014

Walter Stickle is back in this exciting, alien-packed sequel to *Walter Stickle and the Galactic Rangers*!

The parasitic, mind-controlling Goldotti, the most feared creatures in the galaxy, have broken through the containment zone surrounding their home world of Deamus, threatening to spread across the stars like an incurable disease. They will stop at nothing in their mad quest for total domination of all intelligent life.

Only two things stand in their way. One is the most powerful force in the galaxy, a group of soldiers from the planet Argon who will journey to the ends of the universe and back to protect us all. They are the Galactic Rangers. The other is some guy from Pitville, New Jersey, who doesn't even own a car and who thinks it's an adventure to order something other than pancakes at the diner. He is Walter Stickle.

Follow the Galactic Rangers in their latest adventure as they battle the Goldotti and search for lost comrades on the hostile alien world of Gin-Vedra. Follow Walter in his continuing misadventures as he battles his annoying neighbor, Steve "Floodlight" Williams, and searches for better cell phone reception in the most normal town in America. Enjoy the twists, turns, and the surprising conclusion when their worlds collide.

Genre: Science Fiction
Published: March, 2015

The evil Goldotti are gone. The Earth is saved. Walter is a hero. So why is he not living happily ever after? Because the Galactic Rangers, the most powerful force in the galaxy, have been unwittingly creating holes in the very fabric of the universe as their ships travel through the dark space beneath it. Until now, these holes have been too small to have any effect, but an engine malfunction on Scout Ship Gamma has ripped a massive hole in space and time that threatens to destroy the Earth. So once again, the world needs a hero, but has to settle for an ordinary man — Walter Stickle. Follow his adventures in this latest episode as he travels through the hole in the universe to save the world from certain doom.

Genre: Bio-Thriller
Published: October, 2014

Nominated for 2015 thriller of the year by the prestigious Kindle Book Review and finalist for best thriller of 2015 in the IAN Book Awards.

"Only three things in life are guaranteed: you're born, you die, and somewhere in between, if you keep playing the odds, you'll get lucky. What makes me such an expert? Nothing really. My name is Bam Matthews, I'm an FBI agent, and in forty-eight hours, give or take, I'll either be damn lucky or stone-cold dead. Guaranteed."

And so it goes for Bam Matthews, an FBI agent at the end of his career, who in his own words "should have retired years ago, but other than my job all I've got is a dog who can beat me at checkers, an old farmhouse in Jersey with a sixteen penny nail I drove into the kitchen wall to hang my piece at night, and this Gremlin that I've kept running for thirty-six years."

The story opens when a New York hit man comes to town and whacks a local drug dealer right under the FBI's nose. A complicated case to crack, but nothing compared to what Bam and his partner find lying on the sidewalk bleeding to death after leaving the murder scene: the first-ever case of Ebola to be reported in the city. This gritty first-person thriller follows a breadcrumb trail through murder, panic, fear, and revenge, drawing you inexorably to an unforgettable heart-pounding conclusion. As one reviewer said, "You can't put this book down."

Genre: Literary/Gothic Fiction
Published: June 2015

At the bend in the stream on a bristlecone pine, where sage grows wild in fields of mustard and clover, blooms a rose. On a vine wound round the ancient trunk, it waits for the journey to begin in a place far from the stream where the scent of the rose is but a fragrance on the wind and a promise for tomorrow.

With these words, *Transcriber* begins. It is the saga of Benton Doud, a talented young man of little aspiration. It is the tale of his encounter with Jonas White, a sightless, bitter old novelist who has hired Doud to transcribe his final work for him. It is the story of Doud's chance encounter with a mysterious and beautiful woman named

Mary, whose parting gift to him of a rose becomes both his vision and his quest.

Doud's journey takes him to the town of Wenborn, a place out of time where people cling to the old ways and harbor the old superstitions, and where the reclusive Jonas White lives in opulence and solitude. Doud meets many unusual people in the town and at the White Estate, and makes many good friends behind the walls that shelter them from the outside world. But as Doud struggles to please an unpleasable old man, he discovers behind the façade an ancient evil that must be faced if good is to survive.

Transcriber is a story of timeless love and unnatural hate, of all-encompassing good and all-consuming evil, of the things we can see and those we cannot. It is a panoptic vision of a world both natural and supernatural, where life lays out the path and we choose to walk it or not.

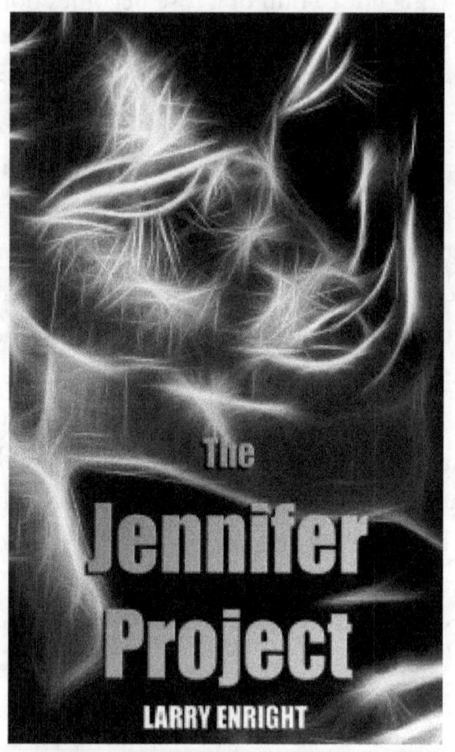

Genre: Science Fiction

Published: June 2016

The Jennifer Project was an Amazon Kindle Scout winner 2016

In 2096, Deever MacClendon creates Jennifer, the first proto-conscious cybernetic processor. It is hyper-intelligent, aware, and evolving. Deever wants to use his creation for the good of all, to help fix a broken world, but knowing what a powerful weapon it could be in the wrong hands, he hides it. When his secret is uncovered, he is forced to plunge into a high-tech morass of deception and treachery to avoid catastrophe and save a world where humans are no longer the most intelligent species.

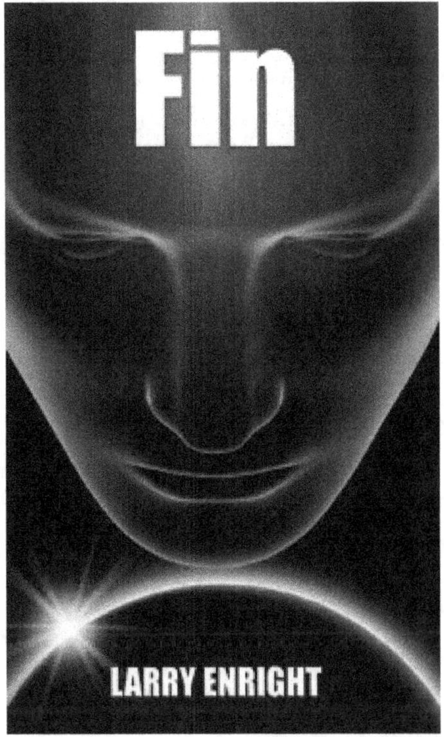

Genre: Science Fiction
Published: October 2018

The year is 402 A.B., anno bellum, the year of the war. The day the Great War began was the day the old world passed into history. They called it the war to end all wars, but it was the beginning of the end. There were so many versions of how it began, who was to blame, who was righteous and who was not; so many conflicting accounts and so much finger pointing that no one knew the truth of it anymore. No one cared. After the first strike and inevitable retaliations, what difference did it make who launched the first missile or which country dropped the first bomb or who was right and who was wrong? Mankind had set the world ablaze. Billions died in seconds. Governments fell in hours. Countries disappeared overnight. Civilization crumbled. After causing the extinction of so many other species, Homo sapiens, the wise man, nearly caused his own. Some said it was a miracle any survived. Others said survival was man's Purgatory; that he hadn't suffered enough for his sins, that he deserved the fate of fighting to his bitter end. This is the story of that end. This is the story of Fin.

Genre: Humorous Fiction
Published: December 2019

What if I told you that the biggest heist in history was one that never made the newspapers, was never seen on TV, and has never even been mentioned in any history book? I'm talking about forty billion dollars stolen. Sounds pretty unlikely, don't you think?

What if I told you that this robbery was pulled off by a bunch of over-the-hill seventy year-olds: a WWI vet who paid his dues in the trenches of Europe, a small-time crook who paid his in installments behind bars, a hotheaded Irishman who thought dues were don'ts, and a giant gorilla who... well... He's a gorilla. Gorillas don't pay dues. Sounds even more unlikely now, wouldn't you say?

Well, here's the kicker. The forty billion dollars I'm talking about was the entire Social Security Trust Fund as of 1972, and funny thing—nobody missed it. It was like it was never there. Now that's totally unbelievable, isn't it?

Well, believe it, because that's exactly what happened. I should know. I was there. My name is Danny Maxwell and this is my story, the story of the Great Social Security Heist.

Genre: Dark Fiction
Published: June 2023

Everyone's got a deal. Gracie's is complicated, but then everything is complicated in the quaint little college town of Holbright. Gracie was born there and has lived there all her life. That makes her a townie, and at any bastion of education atop a holy hill in the middle of nowhere worth its salt, that merits her little more than a look of disdain down a better-than-thou nose. It doesn't matter that she more or less graduated from there or that her father is the college physician. It doesn't matter that she dropped her Holbright twang back in middle school after her latest soon-to-be ex-crush made fun of how she talked. It definitely doesn't matter that she does a better job trimming her nose hairs than they do. A townie is a townie is a townie.

Gracie is not just a townie; she's a townie working through some issues. That explains why she's in a virtual therapy group with three of the other grand-prize winners at this year's Losers at Life awards. They call themselves Stuff. Stupid name, but they do stupid stuff. Speaking of which, one of them is planning on attending Holbright in the fall, so Gracie is giving the group a tour. Unfortunately for her, it's also reunion weekend, a busy time in that quaint little madhouse she calls home sweet home. That's when hundreds of alums get together with classmates they haven't seen or heard from since graduation to exchange conflated memories, drink too much beer, smoke too much pot, and party like there's no tomorrow.

Gracie has managed to survive twenty-four years of reunions mostly just by staying out of the way. This year there's no getting out of the way of the two uninvited guests coming back to Holy Hill for a get-together of a different sort. One is the past. The other is the truth.

REMOTELY ANNOYING

a play in 3 scenes

Genre: Play (Comedy)
Published: July 2023

This 1 hour, 3 actor, 3 scene comedy is meant to be enjoyed with friends around the dinner table after a good meal and plenty of libations.

The premise: The two main characters, Albert and Larry, are 80 year-old twins who have been picking at each other all their lives. They share an apartment, have just purchased a new TV, and are having some difficulty getting it to work. Sounds simple, but things go downhill fast from there and eventually off the cliff when the landlord arrives. The play has a lot of quick back-and-forth dialog so it reads like a comedy routine. It can be performed sitting around the table if someone is reading the stage directions. Actual age of actors is not important.

Minimum props required: TV remote, cell phone, two pieces of paper with Awww! and Clap! written on them, two foldout brochures of any kind to function as TV Quick Start Guide and headphone guide. The rest can be mimed.

If your plan is to perform it onstage, go for it. You have my blessing as long as you credit the work. Posting a review with a pic of the production would be possibly hilarious, but definitely cool.

Reviews: The Lansdowne Times might call Remotely Annoying the funniest thing since sliced bread, but nobody thinks sliced bread is funny and there is no Lansdowne Times. However, this play has been fully tested and approved by 8 brave souls who, shall they rest in peace, died laughing.

Once Upon a Phone

LARRY ENRIGHT

Genre: Family Fiction
Published: November 2024

Hi. I'm Amelia. I live in a tiny fishing village called Hook by the Sea. My dilemma is I'm ten, and I really need a phone, but my parents can't afford it, even if it counts for two birthdays and a Christmas, and even if they never have to give me another gift ever again! So, there's only one thing to do: find a job and buy it myself. I know it'll be tough, but I can do it, and along the way, maybe we'll both learn a little about determination, disappointment, friendship, and love.

Once Upon a Phone first appeared as a twenty-eight-episode serial on Kindle Vella. Hence, the episode titles, numbers, and original notes from the author intended to keep you reading. If you've already read the story as a serial, you may be bored with this book because it's a compilation of the twenty-eight episodes you've already read, unless you're forgetful like me. Then, it just sounds strangely familiar.